THE SURVIVALIST SAGA CONTINUES by Sharon Ahern

Over the years, we've gotten a lot of people asking if THE SURVIVALIST story could continue since not all the threads have been woven shut. We were involved in so many other projects, that while the interest was there for us, the time required was not. One of the biggest hurdles involved was getting the rights back from the publisher in order to use the character names and events. This hurdle was not cleared for a matter of years but, it finally happened. The paperwork was put into the file cabinet and we went on with our other obligations.

About a year ago, Jerry and I started talking about what the Rourke Family could be doing now that their individual families have grown in size and much of their still existing world seems to have grown more peaceful. The Rourkes were just not the type to settle into a retirement village, playing Bingo on Friday nights. Danger would follow the "Family" wherever they chose to travel. Where will they go and what type of danger are we talking about? The new storyline has some villains from the past. No, Karamatsov is not returning. At least I don't think so! There will be some new villains, catastrophes and some far out new acquaintances that will keep the Rourkes engaged in their usual endeavor—saving humanity. Add to the mix of mayhem, politics as usual, an ever growing family base, teenagers and family ties being stretched to the limit, some really cosmic intervention...

So, we've got the rights, lengthy storyline and a cast of thousands all ready to go. The decision was made to invite longtime friend and book author, Bob Anderson, to co-write THE SURVIVALIST continuation with Jerry. Bob is a fine writer and has published books such as *TAC Leader: What Honor Requires, Sarge, What Now?, Anderson's Rules* and *Grandfather Speaks*. He is an expert on weaponry and military skills and is an accomplished public speaker. He has been an avid fan of the series for many years and is familiar with the characters and the numerous stories. New readers we hope will discover a truly unique family saga that has tried to prove over the years that morality and a sense of justice are not just words; they are a way of life. This will be an ongoing collaboration with Bob and we're hoping that fans of THE SURVIVALIST will be pleased to continue reading the series and, to enjoy the further exploits of John Thomas Rourke and his family.

THE SURVIVALIST

#30

THE INHERITORS OF EARTH

Books in The Survivalist Series by Jerry Ahern

#1: Total War
#2: The Nightmare Begins
#3: The Quest
#4: The Doomsayer
#5: The Web
#6: The Savage Horde
#7: The Prophet
#8: The End is Coming
#9: Earth Fire
#10: The Awakening
#11: The Reprisal
#12: The Rebellion
#13: Pursuit
#14: The Terror
#15: Overlord

Mid-Wake
#16: The Arsenal
#17: The Ordeal
#18: The Struggle
#19: Final Rain
#20: Firestorm
#21: To End All War
The Legend
#22: Brutal Conquest
#23: Call To Battle
#24: Blood Assassins
#25: War Mountain
#26: Countdown
#27: Death Watch

Books by Bob Anderson

Sarge, What Now?
Anderson's Rules
Grandfather Speaks

TAC Leader Series
#1 What Honor Requires
#2 Night Hawks
#3 Retribution

THE SURVIVALIST

#30

THE INHERITORS OF EARTH

Jerry Ahern, Sharon Ahern
&
Bob Anderson

SPEAKING VOLUMES
NAPLES, FLORIDA
2013

THE SURVIVALIST
#30 THE INHERITORS OF EARTH

ISBN 978-1-61232-974-1

Map of the New World illustrated by Colin Regn
The alien design illustrated by Faith Maltese

Reintroduction

A man with sun shades sitting on a wooden slat lounge chair, on a Hawaiian beach wearing jeans, boots and a leather bomber jacket would have once been incongruous, even laughable. That however would have been before the Night of the War; before the world had changed and mankind was almost obliterated. In this new world Hawaii's climate included frequent rain and not infrequent snow. Often the islands were now under a cloud cover and a sweater or jacket was common.

The climate changes came because of several factors; besides the effects of the nuclear attacks, there had been geological disasters. The much heralded and misunderstood San Andreas Fault had failed; much of the pre-war West Coast of the United States submerged and parts of Nevada and Arizona turned into beachfront property. A previously undetected fault under the Gulf of Mexico's northern coast line had failed and peninsular Florida vanished into the sea. Other continents were similarly affected.

Open ocean currents in the Pacific as well as the Gulf Stream in the Atlantic had been altered and changed forever; altering climatic conditions and creating glacier growth and formations in the northern and southern hemispheres, extending to roughly latitude 35°. In the aftermath of the worldwide holocausts, the map of the Earth has changed considerably. In many areas the ocean levels has risen, in others they dropped and extended the shoreline, but on a planet so drastically changed, little but the geography and climate was different.

The man's name was John Thomas Rourke and he had lost count of battles and injuries suffered at the hands of the enemies of mankind. It seemed that no sooner had one foe been defeated or a threat eliminated, or another incomprehensible problem solved; a replacement sprang up to take the place of the evil he had just defeated. It had all started so long ago; so many losses—so many faces—most gone but not forgotten.

He had survived and now he just sat; he had been sitting for hours; remembering! The Pacific Ocean's waves crashed onto the beach in front of his home on what remained of Hawaii but he wasn't aware of them; he was simply remembering...

His life had always been fraught with danger; Rourke had never figured out whether he had chosen it or it had chosen him. Not that it really mattered, it was what it was. He had faced every challenge. He had seen every disaster through. The end of his world, of his youth, had come and gone; it had vanished. Now the memories came and went like repeated avalanches, each threatening to overwhelm him and send him tumbling and crashing to his death but they didn't, they couldn't. Rourke had already faced death; horrible mind-numbing death many times and each time had beaten it back.

He thought of a conversation he had with his son Michael one night in the Retreat. He had tried to answer Michael's questions about what happened and why it had happened. "Had the Night of the War never come, it's sad to say that the eventual outcome for humanity might have been little different. The economy of the United States, like the economies of other nations, was already severely strained. The possible solutions to ecological concerns, such as the depletion of the ozone layer, global warming and over population were staggering even to consider."

"Trouble was, Son, if anybody did know the answers, no one was telling. And that was just one of the problems facing humanity. There were diseases, there was poverty, there was international aggression—the catalog was almost endless. And fewer and fewer people wanted to be bothered by the problems. It was better to bury oneself in self-indulgence, bury the mind say in ephemeral pleasures and just wait for the inevitable cataclysm."

"In some ways, the last half of the twentieth century was an era of renewed involvement, but only by a comparatively small segment of the population. Some people, out of ignorance or greed, aligned themselves with causes which were deleterious to mankind's welfare. It could have been stopped and several governments actually had begun some plans for man's survival but to paraphrase T.S. Elliot, 'Mankind just went out with a 'bang' rather than a 'whimper.'"

Just before the "bang," particularly in underdeveloped countries across the world there had been massive unemployment, homelessness, starvation and astronomical inflation. Many of their citizens were hungry, homeless, helpless and hopeless. Their alternatives had been few, starve to death like the many laying dead in the streets of disease and hunger or do something about it. Sometimes drastic change is the only way. It was always better to die as a soldier for change than a starving beggar for existence. But it was too late. The options for corrective actions were lost and war loomed.

When that time came—governments, some governments had thought they were prepared; they weren't. Some of the population had survived in facilities under the ocean, others in bunkers, but it had almost been a planet wide extinction of the human race. Such a waste...

On the night the war started and the end of the world began, Rourke was returning home. His airliner had been diverted and crashed-landed. That was when he first met Paul Rubenstein; a bespectacled nerd, a book worm. A geek with no training or abilities except one—he was willing to learn and he wanted to survive. He would do both!

After recovering his personal weapons from the cargo hold of the crashed plane; he armed Paul. Armed with Rourke's pair of Detonics CombatMaster .45 pistols in Alessi shoulder holsters, Colt Python and Colt Lawman revolvers, an A.G. Russell Sting 1-A boot knife, and a shoulder-slinged CAR-15 assault rifle they set out on an impossible mission.

Paul became his right hand man, picking up a German MP-40 machine pistol in one of their first battles; Paul and that MP-40, which he insisted calling his Schmeisser would prove deadly and accurate. A team had been welded together into a fighting and a thinking unit; and without either—neither would have survived and a friendship had been forged. Once, Paul had described himself as John Rourke's "faithful Jewish companion," a reference, of course, to the Lone Ranger and Tonto.

Rourke's keen sight, consequently sensitive to bright light and often requiring him to wear sunglasses even at night, coupled with his experience as a medical doctor, survival and weapons expert and ex-CIA paramilitary operations officer gave him certain advantages. However, Rourke had known the long and deadly search for his wife and children and Paul's parents in Florida was probably doomed from the beginning. He had no choice but to try.

Early in their journeys Rourke and Paul had encountered a serious opponent, Major Natalia Tiemerovna whom Rourke had recognized from one of his own earlier missions. She was Russian KGB and the wife of Vladimir Karamatsov, head of the KGB in America, but the dark haired and beautiful enemy agent had first converted into a friend. Then she became a companion and finally a loved one—though never a lover. Her favorite weapons were a silenced Walther pistol, an M-16 and a Balisong knife, each of which she handled with competence and deadly efficiency.

Throughout their trials, they knew that at any moment another button could be pushed and the ensuing nuclear holocaust would destroy everything. Crossing vast uncharted stretches of a North American Continent that lay in ruins and devastation they had found other survivors. Some were dying and some were innocent, but they had also encountered Soviet occupation troops, post-apocalyptic thugs and villains, biker gangs, mutants, cannibals, bands of outlaw renegade brigands and butchers and even the new President of the United States, Samuel Chambers.

Ultimately they had survived off of luck, skill, tenacity, guts, drive and the ability to plan ahead. In the end, the Russians had solidified their deadly grip on America and created a threat so diabolical the human race itself might not survive; the imminent combustion of the earth's atmosphere into a global mass of deadly flame. In the last moments of 20th Century Earth, Rourke was locked in a death struggle with Vladimir Karamatsov, Rourke's arch-enemy and Natalia's husband.

That last night he and Rourke fought just outside the protective door of the Retreat while in the distance Rourke could see the fire in the atmosphere triggered by the nuclear devastation approaching. "*Kill the bastard,*" he thought as he fired one last time and stumbled inside and hit the switch that closed the door and sealed himself and his family inside. Their cryogenic chambers and a special serum he had stolen from the Russians gave them the incredible opportunity to survive; but in a new world they would not see for 500 years.

In Rourke's mind he figured only a few would survive the Night of the War. He made a decision, setting his chamber to awaken him early—he then awakened his children, Michael and Annie. For five years he trained and taught them what they would need to know in order to survive and then had returned them to sleep. When the Awakening actually occurred, Sarah was devastated to find she had been robbed of her children's childhood; both were now adults. A theft she would never forgive Rourke for.

The planet-wide extinction feared did not occur, but there had been damage, serious damage. The atmosphere had been crippled, but not destroyed. Gradually, those that had survived began to flourish. Entire countries and their governments had simply ceased to exist. Army's failed and the mighty fallen, knocked to their knees but not destroyed. Those that survived realized that the preparations had not been for "the end times" as much as the times of new beginnings.

In many ways this new world was not unlike the one they had lost, there were some similarities. There were still enemies, some new and some old they would have to kill or die trying. Human animals, despots and maniacs, still strove to dominate those who wanted to be free. He had almost lost his son during those first days after the Awakening and he found that a vile and despicable enemy he had thought long dead, wasn't.

They encountered the Eden Project as the remaining shuttle fleet began to land; but not all that returned from space was to their benefit. In fact, one Eden crew member's death within the first 24 hours of their return heralded both a Nazi resurrection and another Soviet madman hell bent on a planet wide domination.

When Russians had kidnapped his daughter, Rourke had tracked them across the hostile frozen Arctic wasteland finding a group of humans, descendants of a community of Icelanders; isolated in a tropic paradise landlocked by ice and snow. Their blissful ignorance of the deadly battles occurring in the outside world was shattered. To remain alive and free he had had to teach them the damnable realities of war and killing and surviving and, rescue Annie.

Rourke's old archenemy, the Russian bastard Vladmir Karamatsov, long thought dead, resurfaced. Karamatsov now possessed a doomsday device that powered the evil lurking in the heart of each man, in order to satisfy his own lusts. He had been stopped but escaped and fled to the blackened wilderness of China with a plan to seize the nuclear arsenal of Communist China which had survived the fiery conflagration of the Night of the War.

It was then Rourke and Natalia had discovered an underwater facility called MidWake where Marines still battled to defend liberty and justice but beneath the sea. Joining forces they discovered Earth's largest space station at the bottom of the ocean that was home to an American Navy. Birthed in science, the MidWake survivors had also been fighters and keepers of 500 years of history. Rourke, Michael, Annie, Paul and Natalia were still fighting ancient enemies while longing for peace in a world without war. Karamatsov would also survive a kill shot from Rourke requested by General Ishmael Varakov, Natalia's uncle, and leader of the Soviet Occupation Forces in America. Varakov many times showed himself to be a patriotic, honorable and reasonable Soviet soldier, who at times helped Rourke to stop some of the more extreme plans of the KGB. Natalia herself sent Karamatsov to hell.

Russian Colonel Antonovich, Karamatsov's second-in-command, however was ready to launch his own assault on the Second City of China; he was still after China's nukes. Facing two apparent omnipotent adversaries, Michael was captured and had to be rescued.

Days had become weeks, the weeks became months and the months turned into years as Rourke battled neo-fascists, learned of the death of his wife Sarah (murdered by his hated enemy Dietrich Zimmer), found the report of her death was false and was driven into a realm of darkness. As he was about to destroy Zimmer, Rourke was attacked by an unforeseen enemy and almost died.

The saga had lasted over 650 years during which he had met, fought and vanquished the enemies of humanity in every form and shape that damnation could send his way. One Doomsday plot after the other had plagued him, battle after battle, trial after trial culminating finally, unexpectedly in victory.

Sarah had married Wolfgang Mann, President of New Germany, with Rourke's blessing. Michael had married Natalia, Annie had married Paul and he himself had married Emma Shaw a beautiful, competent and cocky fighter pilot. There had been blessings, unexpected but blessings all the same; he had won a victory.

A victory that he had courted, a victory he had sought—but one he had never truly believed was possible. The history of his challenges and battles had been recorded. The legacy he had given to the world was now taught in schools, but he remained uneasy, restless. Too many times he had won, only to find himself thrust into unexpected territories against unexpected and often times incomprehensible enemies, to ever truly relax his guard; but for a few moments he had rested.

Shaking himself from his reverie, seeing the ocean and the water birds for the first time—in how long? Glancing at the Rolex on his left wrist he realized it had been too long. He shrugged his shoulders to let the double Alessi shoulder holster with the Detonics CombatMasters find their usual positions. Unconsciously, his hand passed over the A.G. Russell Sting A-1, as always in its usual place. Turning, he finally noticed the surroundings; clean sand, sparkling waves and the sprinkling of clouds overhead.

"Today is a good day," John Thomas Rourke said aloud feeling both peaceful and rested. He pulled his Zippo lighter from his watch pocket and from a stainless steel flip-top cigar case in his jacket, pulled one of the new thin, dark cigars he had cultivated, cured and recently had started smoking; on rare occasions. Rolling the striker wheel on the Zippo he put the yellow-blue flame to the tip of the cigar and puffed. When the cigar was going to his satisfaction he flipped the lighter closed, stuck it back in the watch pocket of his jeans and turned.

At that moment, a chill came over him and a shadow seemed to pass over him, but looking up he frowned, there were no clouds between him and the sun. No birds passing. He wrote it off to coincidence; after all, tomorrow he and Emma were to travel to what was New Germany for a special presentation then on to the Mediterranean on an archeological dive. All was good, what could go wrong? Then he frowned, "Who knows what can go wrong?" he said aloud. "I need to plan ahead!"

Map of the New World

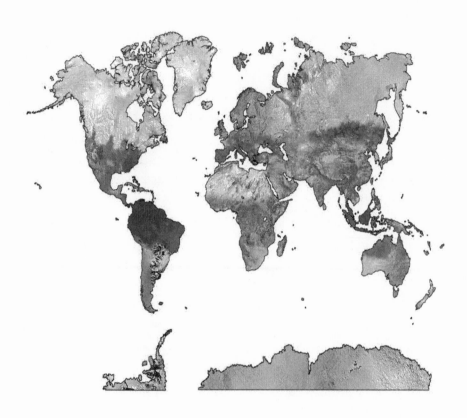

A long, ragged burst from an AK-47 struck the segments of fuselage behind which John Rourke crouched. Whoever commanded the six man KGB unit wouldn't like that. Rourke rolled left, the borrowed HK-91 coming to his right shoulder as his left shoulder impacted the snow and whatever lay under it. He fired once at what looked to be a man's leg, firing twice more before pulling back as the snow rippled under the impacts of more automatic weapons fire. Rourke drew the rifle up close to him, seventeen rounds remaining in its magazine, three spare twenty-round magazines in the pockets of his borrowed parka. The Russian personnel were more heavily armed. As if punctuating his thoughts, bursts of automatic weapons fire peppered the snow on both sides of the wreckage. Rourke stayed as close to the fuselage as he could, knowing his adversaries had no desire to intentionally damage the fuselage or anything associated with the crash.

John Thomas Rourke had no idea of the specific nature of the KGB unit's orders, although he could guess and felt he wouldn't be far off. But, he knew his own orders and—however reluctantly—would follow them, even if something irreplaceable were lost in the process.

David Roth had followed protocol to the letter. The moment the Russian "working group" had arrived on site and opened fire, he'd accelerated the fire engine red snow tractor into a ragged U-turn and driven off. Roth had photographic evidence of the crash site—actually, video tape—and all the artifacts and tissue and blood samples. These could not be lost, regardless. Rourke had to somehow get the best of the six Russians who had come for the same thing he had, and do it quickly enough that Roth would still be in the equivalent of CB-radio range and could somehow be convinced Rourke was not being made to speak under duress—and come back before the night fell upon the snowfield and the temperatures dropped and Rourke would have to use all his survival skills just to live through until morning. Without a vehicle or dog sled—or, even snow shoes—making it forty miles back to the Suburban in near blizzard conditions with the limited supplies Rourke had on his person wasn't likely. If he succeeded in killing the six Russians, he could always steal their snow tractor, unless one of them blew it up, the latter probably being the case.

John Thomas Rourke had always prided himself on paying attention to the detail which could enable him to succeed, his catch phrase, "It pays to plan ahead," something he wouldn't have minded having on his gravestone. The irony of those words under such circumstances would be interesting, at the least.

Realistic planning ahead at the moment would have included serious thought about making his peace with God. Six to one odds and, more importantly, his adversaries' likely hundreds of rounds of 7.62X39mm ammunition and whatever else they had with them against the fifty-seven rounds of .308 Winchester Rourke had on body did not bode well for a favorable outcome. Rourke popped up and fired three quick shots over the fuselage, then ducked down behind it again. Fifty-four rounds. Beneath the borrowed parka and above the borrowed Wooley Pulley, he wore the double Alessi shoulder rig with his twin stainless Detonics CombatMaster .45s. There was a Milt Sparks Six Pack on his belt; but, combined with the magazines in the CombatMasters themselves, that only gave him forty-eight rounds of pistol ammo, not upping the odds even close to favorable.

John Rourke rarely used profanity. But, as Soviet rifle rounds plowed through the snow and drifted near to the fuselage, he couldn't help but feel that the word "clusterfuck" best described the situation...

Chapter One

The mission he was returning from had been satisfying, not earth-shattering but, not everything that was construable as "doing good" had to be on a grand scale. Rourke, three CIA contractors and half dozen Columbian soldiers, had freed fifteen prisoners from Communist narco-terrorists. There was no truly accurate guess as to how many innocent hostages were being held for ransom by the FARC in remote camps in Columbia. For decades, the Fuerzas Armada Revolucionarias de Columbia had financed its war with the legitimate Columbian government through drug dealing and ransoms, some hapless victims spending years in captivity. The fifteen hostages had only been singled out for rescue because one of them happened to be the niece of a United States Senator, and the mission only even possible because a village priest had spotted the blond haired girl.

Rourke, the three contractors and the six Columbian army personnel had approached the FARC encampment from the north, helicoptered in some fifteen miles deeper into the mountain jungles than the camp itself; in that way able to come at the camp from the least guarded direction.

The furthest out guard post was about a mile—everyone else in the hastily assembled unit referred to the distance as two "clicks" or "kilometers—from the camp itself. There was no designated marksman, nor was there a dedicated long range rifle. Rourke had worked his way in as close to the guard post as he dared—he estimated the distance to be three hundred yards. Since he had no idea how this particular M-16 he'd been given would shoot, he couldn't risk a head shot, because he might miss. He'd have to go for multiple hits on center mass.

It was a one-man post. There would be radio checks—that was only common sense—and, if no one answered or someone responded improperly to preset code phrases, personnel would be sent out in force and the entire encampment would be on alert and the hostages might even be moved or worse.

Rourke settled himself on a small outcropping of rock, examining his surroundings to ascertain that he wasn't likely in mid-squeeze to be interrupted by something nasty. One of the contractors—Moises Ortega—served as Rourke's spotter. There was no scope on the M-16, but the contractor had binoculars.

"Can you see him, Rourke? He's coming across that little clearing."

"I see him. His upper body's not turned toward me. He's too skinny a target. I have to wait."

"He's just standin' there. Shit."

Rourke whispered, "The guy seems to be looking around and up at the sky. Anything you see?"

"Naw—wait! Shit, it's his replacement! We're fucked."

Rourke closed his eyes for a moment. He was never much taken with people who used a limited range of profanity to cover up an even more limited range of vocabulary. He opened his eyes. "Moises, here's what you do. When the relief checks in, he'll have to make some sort of radio contact. Let him. The guard being relieved will want to be on his way pretty quickly, since he's got a mile walk through the jungle and the terrain is pretty steep. Get on your radio and get one or the other of the two contractors and two of the soldiers to head him off—just like in the western movies. As he walks down the trail, intercept him and kill him silently. You think one of your guys can do that?"

"Halstead's as good a knife man as I've seen. Yeah," Moises Ortega responded.

"Make it happen. Once the guard being relieved is dead, I'll kill the relief. Have Halstead or one of the guys with him radio you when the guard being relieved is dead. If I shoot the replacement beforehand, the other guy might get on the radio and alert the camp."

"Gotchya, Rourke," Ortega said.

Rourke kept watching across his sights. Of course, he had several perfect shot opportunities, but couldn't take them. He felt the corners of his mouth raise slightly in a smile. He looked away, closing his eyes.

"Okay. I got Halstead and a couple of soldiers in motion, so they can cut the guy off. The replacement's just about to break into the clearing. See him?"

"I've been resting my eyes. Now I see him." A fly loudly buzzed Rourke's right ear. The sun was bright. Rourke took the dark lensed aviator style sunglasses from the pocket of his light blue shirt, squinted, then put them on, his eyes instantly feeling less strained. He had always been light sensitive, giving him far better than normal night vision, but dictating the use of sunglasses more often than most people needed them.

Rourke watched the next person he was going to kill as he—thankfully, not a she—handed over some sort of message to the man he was about to replace. There were many women in the FARC.

Rourke observed as the two men seemed to exchange some sort of pleasant-ry. Largely, Rourke was guessing. He could only identify gross movement at the distance.

The man who'd been replaced started out onto the trail his replacement had just traversed. After a moment or so, he was out of sight in the jungle.

Rourke waited, the lenses of his sunglasses staining with drops of perspira-tion. He set the rifle down, wiped his forehead with a bandanna and breathed on his glasses, then wiped them as dry as he could. He closed his eyes against the sunlight.

"Rourke. Our guys see him. Halstead's gonna take him out."

"Let me know when—exactly." Rourke cheeked the rifle again. He des-pised truly hot weather, and jungles—even high mountain ones—were factories for heat and humidity. Rourke tugged the bandanna from the hip pocket of his faded blue Levis. He wiped his brow for the last time. He smiled, thinking back to medical school and his internship. If he'd been readying himself to cut into a living person, a nurse would have given his forehead a wipe. No nurses were readily at hand and, likely; most nurses would have thought that what he was doing—waiting to long distance another human being—was wrong, possibly evil.

Rourke put the glasses in his shirt pocket, cheeked tightly to the M-16 and moved the selector.

"Rourke! Halstead got him!"

"Protect your ears," Rourke advised, taking a deep breath, letting out part of it, steadying himself. He'd have to ever-so-slightly lead the man he was about to kill, as the man was walking toward the edge of the small clearing. "He's going to take a leak, which means he'd be on edge to me. I'll get him as soon as he turns around."

The man who was about to die watered the plants and turned around. Rourke fired three rounds, stitching them from the man's sternum into the man's throat. As the man crumpled to the dirt, Rourke stood up and put on his sunglasses. "We'd best hurry. Chances of the encampment hearing three moderate reports at a mile distance through heavy foliage are slim to none, but we don't want to take any chances. Let's move. Tell Halstead and his guys to search for any documents, secure all weapons and get themselves up to about a quarter mile—a half a click—from the FARC camp. Get the rest of the guys to check the man I shot for documents and stuff and we'll meet them on the trail. Quickly," Rourke advised.

They'd moved single file along the jungle trail at a fast paced commando walk, little worried about mines and snares, since the path was well worn down between the guard post and the camp itself. As Rourke and the bulk of the force moved silently along the trail, he had two men get about a hundred yards ahead, who would stop when they were up even with Halstead and the two soldiers with him who'd become the de facto advance guard.

More careful the closer they came to the FARC camp, when Rourke, Moises Ortega and the soldiers reached Halstead's position, they resorted to whispers and hand signals. Halstead had—wisely—been studying the encampment, timing the guards' movements. Rourke hauled out the photos taken by the re-tasked satellite, matching physical features of the encampment as shown in the photos to the reality that lay before them.

Rourke assigned two of the soldiers to counting heads and both men, after fifteen minutes, came up with thirty-eight FARC personnel, of the number nine of them women. Rourke was sexist enough to avoid killing women, when he could; but, women pulled triggers as well as men and often better. From the satellite photography, taken over the course of several days and at various times of day, it seemed clear that female hostages were being held in a long green tent halfway between what looked like a privy and a guard post. Male hostages were held on the other side of the encampment, near a meandering stream and an obvious cook tent.

The number of FARC personnel indicated that, as hoped for after setting out bait in the form of a weapons convoy, much of the FARC force was away. The weapons convoy was a fake, to draw as many of the FARC personnel away from the camp as possible. It had worked.

Rourke ran his plans through his head once again. Halstead and the third contractor, Billings, would position themselves to guard the two tents occupied by the hostages, Halstead and Billings each equipped with electric mini-guns. Rourke, Ortega and the six soldiers would be positioned in pairs strategically ringing the camp. At a pre-arranged time, rocket propelled grenades, rifle grenades and automatic weapons fire would be used against the thirty-eight FARC personnel. In the American old west, when an attack such as this was conducted, it had sometimes been called a "murder raid." But, since the goal of this action was a far loftier purpose, the name wouldn't apply, Rourke told himself, smiling.

Rourke and one of the Columbian soldiers, Corporal Canales, took up their position. The sun was still very high and very warm. The young man was sweating, but not from the heat, Rourke realized. He clapped the fellow on the shoulder and whispered, "Just keep telling yourself if we don't kill these people, the hostages they're holding could die here, never see their families, their friends, never live their lives. We're not killing people; they just look like people. The humanity is gone."

In almost perfect English—Rourke had heard Canales speak earlier on—the young soldier said, "I know, Señor Rourke. But, it is good to hear you tell me what you told me."

Rourke nodded. He eyed the black face of his Rolex, watching as the sweep second hand came toward the inverted triangle that was the "twelve." Rourke and Canales each raised their rocket propelled grenades. Rourke glanced at his watch face, rasping, "Now, Corporal!"

Their RPGs fired almost simultaneously into clusters of FARC personnel, six other RPGs firing at the same time. Body parts, dirt, weapons and foliage flew upward, crashing to the ground as Rourke and others opened fire with their M-16s, picking still moving targets. As any of the FARC moved toward either

5

of the hostage tents, the electric mini-guns Halstead and Billings wielded segmented the FARC personnel into unrecognizable chunks.

The raid took under three minutes, but freeing the startled and confused hostages consumed almost fifteen more minutes, Rourke counting the seconds, unable to convince himself that someone in the encampment or one of the perimeter guards to the south, east or west had not somehow alerted the main body of the FARC from this encampment, or another of the FARC encampments not far away.

Rourke ordered, "We're out of here in two minutes. Anyone who can't walk will have to be carried. Canales! Take three other soldiers and rig up some litters." Rourke lit one of his thin dark tobacco cigars with his battered Zippo.

An hour into their trek toward the extraction point, Rourke sent one of the soldiers up into a tree, as high as he could climb. The young man had signaled back that they were being pursued. The only way back from the FARC encampment to the extraction point involved a Burma bridge, crossing over a fast moving stream. One of the freed hostages had lost her footing, fallen and been carried away in the current. Gear and all, Rourke jumped from the rope bridge and dove in after her. He'd slipped out of his pack once he'd hit the water, but his twin stainless Detonics CombatMasters in the double Alessi shoulder rig had stayed with him for the swim.

Rourke caught up with the terrified woman—the one belonging to the Senator—and got her to the opposite bank. Rourke walked upstream, waded into the current and retrieved his pack. There was time for nothing more than pouring the water out of his pack and continuing the escape, FARC personnel hot on their trail. They'd reached the extraction point after a brief firefight with lead elements of their FARC pursuers, and then had gotten everyone out by helicopter.

*****

Later that evening, in his hotel room with a solid meal under his belt, Rourke had detail stripped the Detonics CombatMasters, using only the slide stops to begin the process, needing no other tools. The same could be accomplished on an ordinary 1911, but not as easily as with a CombatMaster. Using Break Free CLP, he'd re-lubricated, and then re-assembled the guns. The Alessi shoulder rig he'd carefully dried with a hair dryer he'd purchased earlier for the purpose. When the leather was nearly dry, he'd placed the CombatMasters in the holsters, so the leather would finish air-drying around them. He'd lit one of his thin, dark tobacco cigars, and then sat in a chair by the window, watching the lights of Bogota's business and entertainment district for a time.

The television incorporated a music only channel. He tried it and, to his delight, one of Antonio Carlos Joabim's magnificent sambas was playing, then still another played after that. He didn't question his musical good fortune as he returned to his chair by the window, lit a second cigar and continued reading the copy of Gun World Magazine he'd picked up when he'd changed planes in Miami, on the way down.

*****

Rourke had been contacted "in transit" while returning from the job in Latin America, picked up at Atlanta's Hartsfield and driven in a police car—sirens, flashers and all—to Dobbins Air Force Base, just north and west of the city. He'd almost felt like a kid again. From Dobbins, he'd been flown north and west to an airbase quite near the Canadian border. That flight was a uniquely memorable experience, Rourke never having flown in an SR-71 before, albeit the aircraft was an SR-71B trainer.

He'd ridden in the elevated instructor's mid-fuselage cockpit and realized two things. First, he would never forget the experience of flying in the famous Lockheed Blackbird, the fastest plane in the world, by all accounts. Second, whatever he was supposed to do when he got out of the plane had to be of extreme importance, in order to merit the cost and speed of the transportation.

Rourke considered himself either on a fool's errand or privy to what may well be the most important discovery in the history of mankind. Ever since he was a kid Rourke had been told he was smart and a quick study, snaring a perfect 45T Score on the MCAT (Medical College Admission Test) and 1600 on the SAT. Had he done poorly on the MCAT, he was prepared to deepen and broaden his casual but abiding interest in astronomy and what lie beyond Earth, and aim his academics at the Astronaut Corps. Because of this never realized bent, Rourke had acquainted himself—as much as allowed—with the generally disappointing findings of Project Bluebook and its antecedent, Project Sign, as well as the Roswell Incident and the supposedly top secret projects at White Sands.

There were still persistent rumors concerning Hangar 18, either the one at Area 51 or the one at Wright-Patterson. He'd even learned much of what could be gleaned concerning Majestic Twelve and the rumored UFO crashes and other incidents which Rourke felt were generally too fantastic to be believed without a great deal of proof—which, if it existed, was unavailable to him.

He was reminded of a famous remark attributed to Napoleon. "History is a set of lies agreed upon." He knew the last leg of this trip was not going to be unique.

*****

The low end temperature range for Break Free CLP was minus fifty-eight degrees Fahrenheit. Conventional lubricant couldn't be trusted at the temperatures Rourke was about to be experiencing, and he still had to go further North. Wind chill was only a factor on living things, of course, flesh and blood—not machines. The wind chill factor was something Rourke didn't want to dwell upon, however.

"How much longer until we reach that spot you showed me on the map, Cal?" Rourke asked the man behind the wheel of the four-wheel drive Chevy Suburban.

"Not much longer, Doctor Rourke."

"It's 'John,' Cal," Rourke reminded the considerably younger man. Cal French was an ex-Army Intelligence sergeant who worked as a contractor for the CIA. Many contractors had some of the highest security clearances, of course, but Cal's apparently wasn't high enough for this mission, one that

Rourke had determined would be his last assignment before resigning his position as a Case Officer in the Central Intelligence Agency. He'd decided to resign while listening to "Desafinado" and smoking a third cigar back in Bogota. Ostensibly, he'd be resigning in order to devote his full energies to writing about and teaching survival skills and weaponcraft. But, more importantly, it would be a way, he hoped, to spend more time with his wife, Sarah, and their two young children, Michael and Annie, at their home in rural northeast Georgia—hopefully saving his crumbling marriage to Sarah in the process.

Once Cal stopped at the co-ordinates they'd both checked on the map, it would be Cal's job to keep the Suburban from freezing up while waiting for Rourke to return from what was either a fool's errand or the potentially most momentous discovery in human history. He didn't know which to hope it was. The orders he'd received when the SR-71 landed had sounded like the set-up for a science fiction movie. Depending on what he found, he might not be allowed to leave the CIA alive. But, he'd cross that bridge when and if he came to it. If there were anything to find at all, he might be in on the prelude to global destruction or a new age—maybe both.

Spending his adult life preparing for the violent collapse of civilization, which he'd always seen as almost inevitable, hadn't been easy on Sarah at all. She was the classic liberal, her pretty head in the sand. Sarah found even the contemplation of what she laughingly parodied as "…the end of civilization as we know it" abhorrent, let alone preparing for it.

Rourke sat in the Suburban's front passenger seat on his way into a near blizzard because of a CIA mole in the Soviet KGB. The man had alerted his CIA handlers that Soviet radar had detected an unidentified object crashing in the northernmost reaches of the common border between The United States and Canada, in the most remote part of Yukon River Valley, an area once disputed between the USA and Canada. Canadian authorities, supposedly, knew nothing of the suspicious object. In a rare example of interagency co-operation, NSA had confirmed Soviet chatter concerning a hastily assembled "working group" that included the KGB's top UFO expert, Vassily Batrudinov.

The snow fell relentlessly, a howling wind from the North blowing it into drifts several feet high in many areas along the dirt track Rourke and Cal traversed. That the Suburban was still on what passed for a road at all was attributable both to Cal's driving skills and Divine Intervention, Rourke thought.

"Any chance I can ask, John, what's this is all about? I got a phone call, telling me to call in on the Covert Operations secure line and ask for Mary. The Covert Ops Director's Secretary?"

"I know Mary. She's a tiny thing. Good hearted person."

"And, she'd tell me the assignment," Cal pressed. "She gives me this laundry list of stuff I need to round up and do and told me where the snow tractor guy was going to meet you and—"

"And, Cal," Rourke grinned, cutting him off, "I'd say you did a darn good job."

"So, ahh—I don't get to know a thing."

"I'll tell you this, Cal," Rourke began. "What we're doing is either going to be quite important or totally stupid."

"What do you bet on, John?"

"The smart money's on totally stupid; but, I'm not a betting man, anyway. Life's enough of a game of chance."

"Will you at least tell me?" Cal asked. "I mean, if it's quite important or totally stupid?"

Rourke laughed. "Yeah; but, if it's 'quite important,' I probably won't tell you. Great job we've got, isn't it?" Rourke laughed again.

Cal lit a cigarette. Rourke very much wanted to light one of his thin, dark tobacco cigars, but the smell of a cigar in a car with the defrosters blowing and the driver and passenger side front windows each cracked less than an inch would have become unpleasant relatively quickly. He wouldn't have smoked at all; but, since Cal hadn't asked before lighting up, Rourke mentally shrugged and asked, "What are you smoking, Cal?"

"Ohh! Sorry, John." Cal extracted the pack of cigarettes from his coat pocket. Unfiltered Camels. Rourke didn't particularly care for cigarettes, but felt Camels were the best to be had. He took the offered pack, shook out a cigarette. "Need a light, John?"

"I'm good." Rourke rolled the striking wheel of the battered Zippo under his right thumb, watching the laboring windshield wipers over the lighter's flame.

Rourke inhaled, exhaling as he said, "If we don't get there soon, pull over and I'll get out and get some of that snow off the windshield." The snow was falling faster and colder than either the windshield wipers or the defroster could keep up with.

Racing sled dogs could travel at better than twenty miles per hour, Rourke knew, sustaining that pace for twenty miles or better. Once the Suburban stopped at the rendezvous point, no sled and dogs would be waiting—only a man and a machine, the man apparently with a security clearance more or less equivalent to Rourke's own TS/SCI Access rating. Rourke and the other man would still have another forty miles to go before they reached the suspected crash site. A dog team would not be quick enough to beat the Soviet "working group," if, indeed, there were one. With a typical ten-dog team, one could cover the forty miles in two and one-half to three hours, without risking pushing the team. With a snow tractor, they could cover that distance in less than two hours easily and have sufficient room to bring back anything they could from the possible crash site. Wind chill—he couldn't help but think about it. Blizzard conditions killed. With a snow tractor, all other factors being equal, although he might be a bit more conspicuous, he'd have a better chance of getting out alive.

Rourke guessed they had about another ten more minutes before reaching the rendezvous. He ran a mental checklist. A rifle he would have neither time nor opportunity to test would be provided for him. A knife larger than his A.G. Russell Sting IA Black Chrome would be available. There would be emergency food and Thermos jugs of water and coffee. He reminded himself to urinate before getting underway again...

Chapter Two

The vehicle was red—not exactly inconspicuous. The extremely tall, skinny looking man standing beside it and shouting over the howling wind told Rourke, "It's a 1972 Snow Trac ST 4. It's got a flat 454 horsepower air cooled VW engine. Great machine! Drives just like a pickup truck—more or less."

The Snow Trac was fully tracked, the sort of thing used to clear ski runs and well suited to more or less flat terrain. Importantly, the cab appeared to have great visibility. "I'll show you the controls, in case something happens to me. We've got plenty of fuel. Any idea what we're supposed to look for at the co-ordinates?" The man's name was Dave Roth, his speech just a little Canadian sounding. Rourke guessed the man was a contractor, like Cal, but had the high enough clearance that he could see whatever was out there.

"Dave, I'm supposed to tell you when we're nearly there. And, after we're in route for a short while, I'm supposed to give you the final numbers for the co-ordinates. This is either pretty important or the guy who's planned the operation is some asshole who reads spy novels too much. So, bear with me on this. Rifle and gear in the cab?"

The tall, thin man opened the door and Rourke stepped inside, Dave Roth right behind him. It was pleasantly warm out of the wind, albeit the Snow Trac trembled slightly just then in a heavy gust. Rourke opened his parka and shrugged out of it. Rourke noticed Roth eying the Detonics .45s. "Best I could do rifle wise was this." Roth reached over to the rear of the cab and produced an H-K 91, the semi-automatic version of the G3 battle rifle. A dozen twenty-round magazines—obviously filled—were in a brown cardboard box the man lifted off the floor to show Rourke. "A couple of extra boxes—twenty-rounders—of ammo, too. Food, Thermos jugs, a First Aid kit. There's a radio on the dash—there. It's on one of the standard frequencies; so, be careful if you have to say anything en Claire."

"I like H-K rifles. What kind of weapon you have?" Rourke asked, ignoring Roth's admonition concerning communications security.

"Same thing. In the box there. If the Canadian government stumbles onto us, though, we're somewhat fucked, Doctor Rourke."

"Call me John. Why?"

"I can maybe talk us out of problems with the rifles. Your handguns? They can mean trouble this side of the border."

"Well, we'll just have to try to avoid trouble, won't we?" Rourke changed the subject. "Navigation?"

Roth laid out maps…

*****

The wind howling, near-blizzard conditions surrounding him, Rourke trudged the last quarter mile toward the crash site, his borrowed Heckler & Koch rifle in his right hand, a Geiger counter in his left. With the crash site in Canada, Rourke and the Russians—if there were any—were all violating Canadian territory.

The driving snow obscured almost all signs of anything out of the ordinary. He moved on toward the coordinates, stopping after another few minutes, taking a compass reading. He made it that he had another couple hundred yards or so. Cold, despite the borrowed parka and Wooley-Pulley, Rourke stopped, leaned the rifle against his hip and rubbed his double gloved hands together. With the wind chill, the temperature was already deadly. Off to his right, Rourke spotted a stand of pines. As the wind slackened for an instant and he was teased with momentarily better visibility, Rourke saw that several of the trees on the farthest edge of the stand appeared to have been damaged. Slinging the rifle from his right shoulder muzzle downward and forward, Rourke walked on, leaning into the wind.

As he neared the damaged trees, Rourke stopped, his right leg almost twisting as he stepped into a hole. Catching himself in time, Rourke drew back. The ground dropped precipitously where it shouldn't have dropped at all. As he looked to his left, he understood. The crashing object had gouged out a trench in the ground. Rourke heard nothing from the Geiger counter, but the wind could have prevented him from hearing anything short of a shot. The needle moved but little, a normal background radiation reading. Edging away from the trench—doubly dangerous, covered with snow—Rourke followed along what he presumed to be its edge, contents of the two largest of his jacket pockets clinking.

It was then that John Rourke saw something remarkable. He had seen both of his children born, Lamazed with Sarah. In all his life, the instant of Michael's and Annie's births would always be more amazing than anything he could imagine. What he beheld a mere twenty yards or so from him was nearly that fantastic: major fuselage pieces of a wedge-shaped craft that was unlike any aircraft he had ever seen, bore markings he could not even fathom.

"UFO," John Rourke whispered. He blinked. Rourke had a folding trench shovel in one of the cargo pockets of the parka. He slung the rifle across his back, opened the trench shovel and began to clear snow away from the largest piece of debris, guessing there was a debris field all along the trench.

There was still no sign of the KGB. Perhaps they weren't coming, Rourke told himself, almost laughing. They would be coming. There was no time for subtlety. He was to find whatever he could that could be brought back for study, smuggled out of Canada. For everything else, explosives. He told Roth by radio, "Get in here; do what you can and get back here. Out." The "do" part referred to videography. When he'd received his orders after disembarking the SR-71, Rourke had asked, "What if I find little green men?"

"They probably won't be green," the man in the suit and fedora hat, who looked like a politician had said.

"Okay. Not green, then."

"If they can be returned for study—and, of course, treatment of any injuries sustained, well—remember, Doctor Rourke; it's your medical background that makes you so well-qualified for this mission. You'll have to determine what to do. Your country will support you, whatever your choice. We'd love to study—and help, of course—any survivors, should there be survivors. But, remains cannot be allowed to fall into the hands of our Canadian friends—we don't want them alarmed—or our adversaries. Anything—or anyone—you can't bring back? Well, don't leave anything alarming or incriminating behind, Doctor Rourke." Rourke nodded.

14

Ice spicules stung at his face and pelted his goggles as he surveyed the possible debris field. Roth approached. It was a very good thing Dave Roth had lots of explosives in his snow tractor. Roth started taping, after a moment or two asking, "What's that gray thing?"

Rourke put down his shovel and looked in the direction Roth's camera was pointed. "I believe that's possibly a dead alien life form," Rourke responded after a moment. He picked up his shovel and started carefully picking his way across the debris toward the slender, arm-like appendage. He removed special gloves from one of his pockets, past elbow length, designed for reaching well up into the carcass of an animal. They were elasticized at the top. Rourke followed the arm toward a neck and a disproportionately large head. He felt everywhere he could think of for a pulse or some other sign of life. There was none.

The arm was exposed because some sort of clothing—a coverall, apparently—had partially ripped away. Roth was filming. The alien pilot wore no helmet, his spacecraft apparently all the environment and protection he usually needed. Rourke had a specially prepared medical kit, which would allow him to rapidly take tissue and blood samples. He also took one cornea, the eye large, brown, and soulful-looking. Familiar with a wide range of religious beliefs concerning the afterlife, he left the other, orders be damned.

"Aren't you supposed to get everything you can? Gonna take his head?"

Rourke looked hard at Ross. "No. Start mining the wreckage and take your explosives back as far as you can along the debris field. All one frequency and I'll have the detonator. Time permitting, I'll open the skull and remove the brain—or, as much of it as I can." Rourke started checking as quickly as he could for artifacts. The coveralls had a self-belt. There was a design on the buckle, most reminiscent of the overturned figure eight that stood for "Infinity," but incorporating something eerily reminiscent of the mathematical symbol for "pi."

Rourke cut the buckle off with the hunting knife Roth had provided, dropped it along with earlier recovered small items into what police would reference as an evidence bag. There was no clue as to propulsion system and, with the time constraint; Rourke doubted any meaningful intelligence could be acquired.

Rourke discarded the elbow high over-gloves, removed the outer pair of the double-gloves and donned the more complete protective gear. Like a surgical gown, but with built-in over-gloves that were one with the sleeves and made from considerably tougher material—he guessed it was Kevlar—it covered Rourke from throat to ankles. Rourke pushed down the hood of his parka and put on the face shield with its built-in Kevlar helmet. And, Rourke began work on the alien's brain, murmuring, "Sorry fella." The skull yielded to a battery powered saw—a little larger and definitely more ruggedly built than what Rourke had seen in surgical theaters—and Rourke turned back the skull cap. The number of lobes was the same as that found in the human brain, but the lobes were larger, which could suggest greater intelligence—or, not. Rourke removed and bagged them.

Roth seemed to be finished with the explosives as Rourke looked up. Rourke felt he was finished with the alien's body. He removed the special surgical gown and draped it over the dead alien. As Rourke pulled up his hood and put on his conventional outer gloves, he called to Roth over the howling of the wind. "Why don't you get over here and give me the detonator. You take what I've recovered so far and get back to the snow tractor. Wait for me—I won't be more than a half-hour behind you—and follow protocols if the Russians get here and things get violent."

Rourke helped Roth pack the artifacts, tissue samples, blood samples and the brain, all into a pack pretty much the size of a teardrop rucksack, then Velcroed and zippered the pack to Roth's existing backpack. The surgical tools went in there as well. Rourke had been notified of the specialized gear by the man in civvies who had met with him where the SR-71 had landed, the equipment already stowed in the waiting Suburban. As Roth trudged off for the snow tractor, Rourke reflected that the rumors concerning numerous crashes and retrieval missions might very well be true. Such mission specific items weren't picked up in a hurry at the local hardware store.

Rourke got to work, searching the wreckage for any technical items he could find. Less than ten minutes into his search, the Russians arrived in a snow tractor of their own, also red, in their case the color appropriate. And, the gunfire began...

*****

More gunfire, Rourke was trapped in the safety of the wreckage. Then, there was silence, except for the keening of the wind and the hiss of ice spicules striking the twisted and torn fuselage parts of the alien spacecraft. During the lull in shooting, Rourke surveyed the ship one last time. It would have to be blown up to be kept from the Russians. Even if Rourke were able to somehow get to an even marginally safe distance before detonation, the odds on getting shot down were hard to ignore. He always carried a pocket handkerchief, never liking tissues. He'd taken two extras from his suitcase before stashing the bag in the Suburban with Cal.

Rourke had seen downed aircraft on several occasions. He prided himself on logical thinking and not guesswork, but he couldn't escape the feeling that this craft behind which he'd taken shelter had been shot down, not merely met with an accident.

A voice called out from the KGB position, "I decided to set aside a few moments for our ears to stop ringing, American."

"How do you know I'm not a Canadian?"

"American is my guess and I'll stick to it."

"Right you are, Doctor Batrudinov," Rourke responded cheerily.

There was a pause, then, "And how do you know my name?"

"I've read many of your articles and I admire your work. It is an honor to meet you, sir, even under these circumstances. Who else would the KGB send to a UFO crash site, after all, but the Soviet Union's expert of experts?"

Batrudinov paused again. Perhaps he was being fed questions, or just pensive. "I assume you've already done a great deal of work and that you have the craft set with explosives, to deny it to the Union of Soviet Socialist Republics." Rourke didn't say a thing. After a moment, Batrudinov asked him a question. "Assuming you have placed explosive charges about the craft and are willing to die in order to deny us access, I would ask one simple favor—in case you are successful."

"At blowing up the spacecraft, dying or both?" Rourke asked.

Batrudinov laughed. "Is the pilot a gray, about human height, but with a considerably larger head?"

Rourke looked at the detonator in his hand. "I'm going to have to go in a moment, Doctor Batrudinov. If we both survive, I'll deny I said this. But, he's a gray, as you suggest."

"Thank you, sir!"

"You are welcome, sir!"

"You can just walk away. We will not shoot, unless you detonate."

"I'm afraid I can't do that, Doctor. As I'm sure you have to yours, I've taken an Oath of Allegiance to my Country. Great meeting you!"

John Rourke had planned ahead. Before slipping across the border between the USA and Canada, John Rourke had asked Cal to stop at a liquor store. He'd purchased two fifths of Smirnoff 100. Rourke lit the first Molotov cocktail and hurtled it toward the Russian position. He lit the handkerchief in the neck of the second Smirnoff bottle, hurled the Molotov and dropped his Zippo in his pants. The HK-91 slung muzzle down from his right shoulder, John Rourke was already off at a dead run, trying to keep as much of the spaceship's wreckage between him and the KGB personnel, gunfire already ringing out between the explosions of the Molotov cocktails. Bullets plowed the snow and the ground beneath it, pinged off the occasional errant bit of wreckage, zinged past him, frighteningly close. Rourke kept running.

Rourke had to get at least a hundred yards between him and the wreckage before detonating; and, that could be cutting it close. He kept running, slipping on the snow, nearly falling. Rourke swung the HK-91 forward on its sling, running. His right fist balled on the rifle's pistol grip. He kept running. The gunfire still hammered into the ground around him, but the natural contours of the terrain were helping him to dodge and weave without even trying.

One hundred yards. One hundred ten. Rourke kept running. After the run, if he couldn't raise Roth, Rourke was setting himself up for disaster, working up a heavy sweat as he ran, a heavy sweat that would instantly start to dry and chill him the moment after he stopped.

Rourke flicked the safety lock on the detonator, glanced over his shoulder once as the Russians advanced on the wreckage. Rourke had no desire to kill them all. They were merely doing their jobs as he was doing his. He would miss Batrudinov's musings concerning extra-terrestrial visitation. Rourke found himself wondering what the man really knew, but couldn't say. Rourke flipped the switch. From behind him, he heard a low roar, becoming louder and louder as the charges—set in series—began to explode.

Rourke didn't look back…

Roth had not quite followed protocols, returning when the explosions started, looking for Rourke. Rourke knew men in the Company who would have ratted out Roth, albeit what Roth did turned out for the best.

As he sat at the snow tractor's controls, driving them toward the rendezvous with Cal and the Suburban, Roth suggested, "You know, we could just eighty-six all the stuff from the wreckage."

"And?"

"Do you think they'll have us whacked because the crash was too sensitive?"

Roth seemed genuinely nervous. "I doubt it. I've come to the conclusion this sort of thing happens on a semi-regular basis, hence the specialized surgical gear and the like. No. You stick with the Company and you'll probably be fine. Now, as far as I'm concerned, I was planning on resigning before they grabbed me in transit and drafted me for this. They may not want me to do that."

The CIA had not wanted Rourke to resign and, in the end, Rourke, although he never intended to—nor did—work for the CIA again, was carried on the "active" list. He knew better than to mention to anyone what had transpired at the crash site in Canada. For those he loved, the knowledge was too dangerous.

*****

Vassily Batrudinov survived and, quite some time later, Rourke, on a 747 flying back toward Atlanta after conducting survival training with the Royal Canadian Mounted Police, read a magazine article by Batrudinov. The Soviet expert stated unequivocally that, although his belief in extra-terrestrial visitation was unshakeable, he had to admit that, to his knowledge, no physical evidence had ever been found—at least not by the Soviet Union.

A balding, young man with glasses, sitting not far from Rourke, walked past him down the aisle. Noticing the magazine, apparently, the man asked, "You believe in UFOs?"

"I try to keep an open mind. How about you?"

The younger man smiled, nodded. "Yeah—me, too."

Chapter Three: Over 650 years in the future

Natalia sat in the women's lounge aboard the Presidential deep dive submersible, the vessel mere moments away from Mid-Wake. Adjusting her hat in the mirror, she laughed a little, shaking her head. Natalia and her husband, Michael, dress '40s. In the last several years, it seems, those who could afford to had started dressing as if they are going to a costume party. The young people who dressed '20s looked foolish and the young people who dressed '60s—at least the girls—looked good. As the wife of a possible Presidential candidate and as a mother, mini-dresses would be a bit much—or not enough, depending on how one looked at it. She glanced at her legs, checking to be sure her seams were straight and walked out of the room.

Joining Michael at the front of the craft, they sat together holding hands and watched the Presidential DDS on security camera images being broadcast from Mid-Wake. Once the docking procedure was completed, Michael stood up said, "Okay, my lady, it's show time," donned his fedora and snatched up his E-case. Glimpsing their image in one of the security monitors she remarked, "We do make a lovely family." Standing next to them was their son, John Paul, 12 and daughter Sarah Ann, age 9.

"You're the one that's lovely," he said squeezing her hand. Approaching the security station they pulled out their ID tags for the guard to verify, he nodded and waved them through. "You know, I've been thinking," Natalia said affixing Michael's tag to his lapel, "Having a wife who was at one time a Major in the KGB, could be a detriment to a man with Presidential aspirations."

"Yes, it could," he agreed, "were that lady not looked at as one of the Heroes of Mankind, chief among that illustrious 'pantheon' my father, John Rourke."

"Michael," she said turning serious, "I have to admit I'm worried and Annie and Paul are worried. We are worried that you may have to compromise your integrity in order to get elected President and even to do the job. You know how politics work; it is the art of compromise."

Michael turned on his heel, fixing her with a steely gaze and said simply and finally, "Annie and Paul are wrong..."

Chapter Four

Sarah Rourke-Mann, wife of the President of New Germany had a soft spot in her heart for children. Her old life had started off as a story book. Then the Night of the War had ripped that to pieces and scattered those pieces, never to be totally reclaimed. It hadn't been her husband John's fault, in fairness to him he had done more than anyone would ever really know to find her, Michael and Annie and save their lives.

His preparations, his skills, his sheer tenacity were the only reasons any of them had survived. But that survival had come at a terrible cost to Sarah. After countless battles the end of the world as she had known it had finally come and they entered into a long sleep. When they all had awakened 500 years in the future she found that John's plan, a plan he never discussed with Sarah had robbed Sarah of her children's childhood. When she awakened, Michael and Annie had been awakened before her; long enough to have grown from early adolescence to adulthood. She had missed out on so much. And there was the issue of her third child, a second son named Matthew.

John had been so excited when he learned she was pregnant again, she had thought it was the chance for them to find some type of repair. A new beginning, a child she could watch grow up, the thing that had been denied to her with Michael and Annie. Then came another threat. Sarah delivered Matthew during the Nazi attack on Eden City, led by the bastard Dr. Dietrich Zimmer. Matthew had been ripped from her arms; Sarah had been shot in the head but the saga of Matthew didn't end there. John Rourke had also been injured and both were at deaths door. The decision was made to re-enter the cryogenic sleep in hopes its restorative powers could save both of them.

Upon awakening, Sarah had learned that Wolfgang Mann had given up his old life and had entered the sleep with her. He hoped that if she ever awoke, he would be there to share a new life with her. Instead of killing her child, Zimmer had raised him as his own but had modified baby Matthew's DNA with strands from the monster, Adolf Hitler. Zimmer's mad scheme had played in a way that both saved her life and had doomed Matthew who had grown to adulthood.

Zimmer's brainwashing and genetic manipulations had resulted in a monster, and evil sadistic monster, just like Zimmer.

John Rourke had been forced to kill his own biological, albeit, modified child. Sarah had witnessed it, again Rourke had done what was necessary and Matthew had died, corrupted by a monster. He had been turned into a monster and Rourke had had no choice. Intellectually Sarah knew that and was reconciled to the facts but her emotions were another matter; while she truly loved John—she could no longer live with him.

Wolf's selflessness had won her heart and her hand. The last few years had been filled with peace and a love she knew could never have been with John. Knowing that she could never again conceive a child left her incomplete. There would be no chance to complete that kind of cycle again. Now, she tried to participate in the childhood of others, although it never seemed to fill that horrible longing she knew she could never fill.

In a few hours, her ex-husband John Thomas Rourke was going to step back into her life. While she truly, honestly loved John—it was in a complex and convoluted manner. He was her hero but at the same time she hated him because of Michael and Annie and she could never completely forgive him for Matthew's death. It had been both a terrible but freeing day when she finally admitted she would always have love for John Rourke; she just couldn't live with him any longer. Her love for Wolfgang Mann, now her husband had its own complications, yet it was simpler and more fulfilling than her love for John. Sarah shook her head forcing her conflicting images back into the recesses of her brain.

At the last minute, she had decided to stop at this elementary school to spend a few moments reading to the children before Wolf joined her after picking up John and Emma at the airport before the dedication of the new medical college. She needed a few moments of simplicity and sanity before John Rourke came back into her world. She had called Wolfgang and told him what she was going to do and he had told her, "That sounds like exactly what you need. Enjoy yourself."

She ordered her security detail to the new location and walked into the school unannounced. She had her travel team, only two vehicles and four guards. The team leader was not happy about the change in plan but agreed to it, "Provided we are only there a few moments, Ma'am." Sarah had given her word.

The first ten minutes were absolute joy; she felt so full of life reading to the eager students and taking them to places of wonder and magic. Then a man rushed in and said, "There's been an accident in the parking lot." Two of her guards had gone back out with the man to investigate and if necessary call for help. Less than a minute later, the man returned and while trying to explain some complications to the security detail team leader, he moved closer to Sarah before suddenly pulling a revolver. He grabbed Sarah, ordering the two guards to drop their weapons and lie on the floor.

A loud whistle brought the rest of his team along with the other two security personnel inside. Sarah could tell from the dress of the perpetrators they were neo-Nazis. Skin-headed with Swastika tattoos and patches, the terrorists forced all but one class of third graders to "Leave the building and spread the word, we now hold the First Lady of New Germany." He shouted, "Seig" and the others responded with "Heil" and the straight armed salute that Adolf Hitler made famous during the Second World War.

As a sign that meant business, four of the terrorist casually walked over to where the security team laid face down with plastic zip-ties securing their hands behind their backs. Each terrorist calmly fired a single round into the back of the heads, killing all four of Sarah's security. She knew that the two adults and the children and yes, even Sarah herself were all on their own.

*****

Emma Rourke adjusted the controls of the aircraft she was piloting herself and her husband in as they approached New Germany, in Argentina. A new medical college was being dedicated and named after John Rourke. Rourke, sitting beside Emma in the co-pilot's seat, said, "You know I never did much having to do with medicine, despite being an MD. I was always too busy with other activities or fighting in a foreign country or learning secrets nobody wanted to give me. Why would they want to name a medical college after me?"

With a sideways glance at him, Emma said, "Well, it might have something to do with the fact that, without you, if anyone were still alive in the world, which would be doubtful, those persons would almost assuredly be living under a totalitarian regime. So, stop complaining."

He laughed and fired off a salute, "Yes Ma'am, Sir, I'll shut up. I have to tell you though I'm really excited about going to the coast of North Africa when we leave New Germany. I want to be there when the Team starts bringing up more of the wine and olive oil jars. When they opened the first two and found that they didn't contain wine or olive oil but scrolls smuggled away from the Library of Alexandria, before its contents were lost forever—as the Roman Legions burned it; man what a find. If there are more and they really are from the Library, this could be one of the most important discoveries ever made. Especially those in languages no one has ever seen before, some in Greek, detailing the existence of a proto-human civilization, possessed of highly advanced technology. If we can only decipher what they say."

Emma setting up for the final approach smiled and said, "I am excited my-self and as a child of technology, I'm certain the defense department's computers will do the job. Oh, by the way Dear, I meant to tell you something. I'm pregnant."

*****

As a PhD candidate at the University of Mid-Wake Amanda Welch was researching for her dissertation and combining this with her lifelong passion—genealogy. The University of Mid-Wake was the oldest surviving academic institution on Earth, it was located at Mid-Wake, beneath the Pacific Ocean. Amanda, an indirect descendent from one of the original Eden Project cadre got most of her lineage from Mid-Wake, the experimental underwater colony which survived The Night of The War. Mid-Wake had been able to expand and thrive. It is from Mid-Wake that virtually all of the racial stock of the new United States originated.

Her thesis on theoretical astrophysics had allowed her, as part of the work, to be able to examine the electronic logs of the original Eden Project's five hundred year voyage. Even now, she was amazed they ever made it on their elliptical voyage toward the far distant reaches beyond the edge of the solar system. If she weren't already religious, realizing the perils the Eden Project ships survived without force fields to protect them from the destruction that could have been wreaked upon them by even microscopic meteorites or the chance encounter with almost anything else would have made her a believer.

However, Amanda had found an anomaly. It couldn't possibly be correct, but here it was. She had to call it to the attention of her professor, Doctor Emil Culbertson. After gathering her personal electronics, she glanced at herself as she pulled on her cloche. She's a '20s and loved the look… She made her way from her small off-campus apartment to the meeting with Doctor Culbertson, for which she was already late.

Following the meeting with her faculty advisor and several other doctoral candidates, Amanda left the office, waiting about 30 seconds before cracking the door back open and asking Culbertson, "Do you have an extra minute? There is something I need to show you." Culbertson waved her in, refilled his coffee mug and motioned her toward the large plotting table in the center of his large office. "What do you have, Amanda?" Culbertson liked the spirited and intelligent student, she was articulate with a passion for education—and she was very easy on the eyes.

"Okay, thanks for giving me this time. As you know I have been reviewing the electronic logs of the Eden Project's voyage and I think I have found an anomaly. Now, I know I have something but I can't figure out exactly what it is or what it means or if it means anything at all." Amanda realized she was talking much too fast and inhaled deeply to settle her nerves.

"That is what an anomaly is, my dear. Something that initially we don't understand, we have to study, examine and dissect the data to figure out what it is, if it is anything at all and what it could mean, again if anything at all," Culbertson said gently, he could tell Amanda was nervous.

Taking another deep breath Amanda started again, "It is amazing to me that the Eden Project even made it. Amazing they survived on the voyage into deep space and back from beyond the edge of the solar system."

"Ah, yes," Dr. Culbertson said taking a sip of the black mud he called coffee. "A truly remarkable feat and all without modulated force protection fields; they should have been destroyed by meteorites ranging from infinitesimal to significant, if not heroic size. What is the anomaly?"

"The Eden Project flight, as impossible as it might seem was interrupted and remained in a geosynchronous orbit around something—I have no idea what— for nearly three terrestrial years before continuing on, as if nothing had happened."

"Impossible." Culbertson said emphatically. "That my dear is quite simply, impossible."

An hour later, Amanda took care to simply close Culbertson's office door not slam it shut as she wanted to do, hopefully shattering the window in it as a by-product of her anger. After reviewing the data, Culbertson had tried to disprove her claim and failing that had told her privately that he couldn't counsel her strongly enough to forego any references to the anomaly. "Amanda, you'll make yourself a laughing stock within the scientific community. In less than three hundred more years, it will be the year three thousand. In all of that time, there has never been any even remotely provable example of extra-terrestrial life. Yet, you claim the Eden Project Fleet was stopped for three years, in geosynchronous orbit around something but you can't tell who stopped it and where it was stopped. The reason I say don't discuss the anomaly is, my dear, you are hitching your star to a computer glitch."

Finally, frustratingly Amanda agreed to *consider* dropping any reference to the anomaly but while a budding if beginning scientist, Amanda was also known for having a stubborn streak. Amanda took the Tubeway off campus to the high rise apartment she shared with her girlfriend Paula. It was affordable and that's all that she could say about it originally, but, the two friends had made it homey...

Chapter Five

The press pool covering Rourke and Emma's arrival for the dedication ceremony celebration led by Wolfgang Mann, President of New Germany, and his wife, Sarah, was waiting at the airport. As Rourke and Emma deplaned, one reporter shouted a question to Rourke about Michael running for the Presidency. "Would that not make for a historic alliance between the United States and New Germany, Michael's mother the wife of New Germany's leader?" Rourke simply nodded and pressed on through the throng of reporters and well-wishers to be greeted by Wolf and his presidential security team.

Once inside the airport a uniformed officer approached Mann and whispered something in his ear. Mann turned to the Rourke's and simply said, "Please follow me immediately, we have a problem."

Rourke asked, "Wolf, what is going on?"

"John, we have just learned that a group of neo-Nazi terrorists have seized the school where Sarah was making an unofficial visit. Sarah was reading to a group of small children when the group entered the school. All we know right now is that Sarah, along with a dozen children, their teacher and an assistant teacher, are being held hostage."

"Where was her security...?" Rourke demanded.

"Initial reports are the Security Team's communications were neutralized, we don't know how. The attack was swift, vicious and overwhelming; the security team has been murdered; executed to be more accurate. The terrorist's demands are impossible—even if they weren't; their timeline is. They're threatening to kill Sarah and the other hostages and in 20 minutes will begin to execute one every ten minutes thereafter. Our security plans never anticipated an event like this, there is no way for our regular forces to get here in time."

"Was this a planned and advertised visit to the school?"

"No," Wolf said. "Totally spur of the moment. Sarah only decided to go about thirty minutes before the attack. I was going to pick her up there after I had picked up you and Emma."

"Good," said Rourke. "This had to be a target of opportunity. That means the terrorists did not have a chance to do a thorough analysis of the building plans. That can work to our advantage. How far away is the school?"

"Close to us, maybe ten minutes but too far for my SWAT and Hostage Team; they wouldn't be able to respond and set up in less than thirty minutes."

Rourke laid his and Emma's attaché cases on a nearby table and stripped off his suit coat and popped open the cases. He pulled his double shoulder holster from his cases, checked magazines and ensuring both .45s had a round in the chamber and the thumb safeties engaged, before slipping the double rig on and shoving a CombatMaster into each holster. Then he popped open Emma's case and taking loose his belt, threaded two holstered .357 Colt Pythons in place after checking to be sure the cylinders were full. He pocketed two Safariland speed loaders and handed the shoulder holster with its Sig 226 clone and extra magazines to Emma.

"Wear this, I don't care what Wolf's Security thinks about it, wear it. You are not going." Rourke patted his own stomach, Emma nodded.

Turning to Mann, Rourke's face was hard, "Here's the situation. We have an active-shooter situation, we have hostages; the bad guys have already killed which means they won't hesitate to kill again. We don't have time to wait for re-enforcements; we have to go in now. Wolf there is no other way. Between you and me and your security detail we can do it."

"Excuse me, Sirs," Manfred Schmidt, head of the security team said. "That cannot be allowed to happen. I am sorry but this detail's primary responsibility is to protect the President; I have given orders to local law enforcement to send additional officers to isolate and secure my President at this location, they are en-route as we speak and the motorcycle officers that accompanied our convoy are already establishing a cordon of protection. The other situation cannot take precedence over the President's safety."

Wolfgang Mann, the President of New Germany, one of Rourke's oldest comrades and one of the world's most recognized fighters, slumped and nodded. Rourke knew he was alone. "Wolf, I'm going in if it has to be by myself. There is no option, give me four of your guys. I can do it with four."

"Negative, Herr Generaloberst Rourke that cannot happen. Our duty is to protect the President and that is what I'm going to do."

"Wolf, with four, I can do this. By myself, it is a suicide mission for me and a death sentence for the hostages, one of which I remind you is Sarah. At least give me a sniper, someone to cover me and give me a chance to get in the building..."

One of the security detail members stepped forward, "Herr President. I am a qualified sniper, I have my weapon with me and with your permission I will volunteer to assist Generaloberst Rourke." Schmidt started to object but was silenced by a wave of Mann's hand.

"Thank you Sergeant," Mann said to the volunteer. "I am indebted to you. Retrieve your weapon. John, what else?"

"Can you give me the loan of two of your MP-7s? Second, can you get me close to the school?"

Mann nodded, "The answer to both questions is yes."

"You are to keep Emma with you. Stay in this location and secure it. Is that acceptable Mr. Schmidt?" Schmidt nodded. "Good, I need a vehicle and driver to drive me and the Sergeant near the school and drop us off. Tell your emergency responders to stay close but out of sight until they see my all-clear signal."

Wolf designated a driver, with that Rourke winked at Emma and with his new sniper followed the driver to the parking lot. While in transit, he was able to use the vehicle GPS system to pull up the school's location and view the layout of the neighboring streets for the best approach. "What is your name, Sergeant?"

"Jäger, Herr Generaloberst, Hans Jäger."

"Jäger? Am I correct that means Hunter?"

"Yes, Herr Generaloberst, it does."

"Hans, you and I are going on what well could be a death mission. I'd appreciate it if you would call me John," then extended his hand across to the back seat where the sniper was already adjusting the rifle that would protect Rourke. They shook hands and looked into each other's eyes, a look only people who have been in combat or those about to go into could fathom. Turning back to the driver Rourke said, "Here, drop us here," pointing at the screen.

Five minutes later, Rourke and Jäger were dropped off; the New Germany Security Police had cordoned off the entire area and were beginning to evacuate the nearby buildings. They crossed the security line and began moving toward the school building. Before Rourke turned into the alleyway he stopped and did a quick inventory. Between the CombatMasters and two Pythons he had a total of 68 rounds.

He had the MP-7 slings slung over his neck and one over each shoulder forming an X on his chest and back. He hoped that wouldn't give the bad guys a target to aim at. The MP-7 on his left side was primed and set for fully automatic fire; he would use it for suppressive fire. It, like the one under his right arm was loaded with fifty 9mm rounds, Rourke didn't think it was enough but it was all he had—168 rounds—total. The one on his right was set for semi; he would engage individual targets with it. As their ammo ran out he would simply discard them and switch to the .45s.

The .357s, his last line of offense, unless he could rearm from one of the terrorists he planned to kill. His Leatherman Wave MultiTool rode next to his wallet in his left rear pocket and the A.G. Russell Sting A-1 just behind his right hip bone mounted to the belt. He had wadded up his tie and shoved it in his right rear pocket, maybe a tourniquet or restraint. Looking at his dress pants he grimaced. "Wished I had a pair of jeans, these are not going to last through the next few minutes. While I'm wishing, I wish I had a pair of combat boots but at least I have boots with a decent tread instead of dress shoes." Making one last check of the holster retention straps, he stood.

"Okay, Sarah I'm coming; hang on."

He was hoping the neo-Nazis were in fact not totally familiar with the school building, from the initial reports they seemed to have covered the front of the one and a half story building, expecting the attack would come from there. That would have been logical to expect; Rourke was hoping to surprise them with something illogical, it was after all his only chance. To get a full picture of the building required Rourke and the sniper to approach it several times from different streets. On the third viewing, Rourke saw what he was looking for, next to the loading dock was what appeared to be a garbage chute he hoped the terrorists had not noticed.

They had spotted two terrorists on the roof of the second level of the school to the left providing over watch for the operation. From the far end of the building they had good high ground and almost perfect visibility. They could see and shoot at any threat but he noticed each carried an inexpensive civilian model walky-talky. He knew they had only about a quarter mile range and that was line of sight. In an urban operation like this they would be useless except for communication to the inside of the building.

Rourke's reconnoiter had identified a single weakness; on right side of the ground floor, the garbage chute. If he could make a short rush to that wall without getting killed he had a chance at pulling this off. If he didn't, Wolfgang Mann's Tactical Teams would have to breach the building and clean up his mess, along with—he was sure—his and Sarah's bodies. His concern was that this was beginning to look like an amateur event not a well-coordinated and planned action. However, that could be a ruse, a set up and there could be surprises ready to kill him. There was only one way to find out.

"Hans you have two minutes to get to that third story window right there." Rourke pointed to a building across from the school. "Can you take two shots from that location and remove the sentries without being detected and do it silently?" Jäger nodded and set out at a run to circle to the near side of the building. Rourke figured he had twelve feet to cover and when one of the guards turned to the other and asked for a light for his cigarette, Rourke moved.

Feeling naked during his dash and expecting a shot at every step, he sprinted. Leaning with his back against the brick wall, he steadied his breathing and stared at the window he hoped Jäger was ready in. A window shade moved, twice—Jäger was ready. Rourke stepped up on a convenient water faucet and cautiously lifted the opening of the chute; all the time dreading a fusillade of automatic fire which luckily did not come. As luck would have it the chute wasn't a chute at all. Lifting the cover he saw simply a room with a closed door; smiling at his luck, Rourke pulled himself inside.

Phase one was completed; now came the hard part. Listening at the door, he heard nothing. If there was something on the other side, or someone, the metal door was too think and too well sealed to tell. On one of the shelves he saw a squeeze can of 3-IN-ONE oil. He jerked the red plastic top completely off and liberally poured oil on the two hinges then replaced the can on the shelf. Gently and carefully turning the door handle, the latching bolt cleared the facing plate.

The door opened and through the crack he saw them, unbelievable—they were standing in what appeared to be a kitchen or break room, relaxed, waiting on coffee to perk—five idiots on a coffee break, about to die and with no clue. In the background he could hear children whimpering and a woman crying.

His assessment of the situation changed on the spot. These were not seasoned killers, they had killed certainly and they had done it maliciously and efficiently but there was no weapons discipline in the other room. Three had laid their weapons on the kitchen table half way across the room and the barrels were pointed in all directions; two didn't have their bolts closed. The smell of marijuana hung in the room. One dork, with extreme earrings had his weapon leaning against a cabinet, also out of reach, so he had both hands free to snort a line of what looked like cocaine from the counter top. The last punk, his bleached hair arranged in a "do" that reminded Rourke of Woody the Wood Pecker, had his AK slung over his back and they were joking and laughing about this "great adventure" and how they would be "heroes" of the new Fatherland. Rourke could see no security plan in effect; this changed everything.

Were they vicious? Yes. Were they seasoned professionals? No, these looked like punks who had been pumped up on propaganda and turned loose with a rough plan that could never have worked and now were high on drugs and blood lust. Alright, Rourke eased the door shut and silently counted. If there were only ten, two were on the roof and they were at best a secondary threat and he would be able to see them responding down the stairwell on the other side of the room.

Rourke realized for the first time that he might actually pull this off. It was no longer a case of strategy; it would be a case of slaughter. If he could kill the five in the other room and Jäger could take out the two on the roof that left only three as a primary threat, but the element of surprise would definitely be gone.

Were they professionals, they would execute Sarah at the first gunshot. Rourke's gut told him that maybe he could pull it off; maybe, and that was a big "maybe."

Another big "maybe" was if he had the correct count on the enemy numbers, maybe and maybe not. If the count was off—he was the one about to die and he would die before he was able to save Sarah. The third "maybe" was if he was correct in his assessment of his opponents. If there was a single professional in this group and there could well be, he was in trouble. Yet, often his strategies had been sound, but his gut told him something else. Strategies had occasionally failed him, usually because of something unknown or unpredictable happening that changed the equation. His gut had never failed him and he had learned to trust that gut. His strategy, while well thought out, never gave him much chance in surviving long enough to rescue Sarah and get either of them out alive. Why not go with the gut, stranger things had happened.

Flipping both MP-7s to full auto, he regretted leaving his suit coat with Emma; it held his cigar case and he could sure use one right now. Discarding that useless thought, Rourke gripped the MP-7 in his right hand and worked the door knob with his left; he was ready. It was plausible the first fifteen rounds from that weapon would drop the bad guys. Five or ten more from the MP-7 in his left would keep them down. That would leave another 10 rounds in his right hand to deal with a threat from the front of the school and fifteen to address the jokers on the roof. By that time he would switch to a .45 to finish the rest off, reload and engage the final threat that held Sarah hostage. Not perfect but doable.

It was now or never and in one motion Rourke jerked the door open, began spraying the next room with his right hand weapon, aiming chest high. The first half magazine caught them totally unprepared. Three of them jumped and danced to the impact of the 115 grain jacketed hollow points slamming into their bodies. Rourke pulled the trigger of the MP-7 on his left, opening up with it also.

Woody the Wood Pecker, the punk with his AK slung across his back, was the only one that reacted with any degree of appropriateness. While the other four were bouncing around the room, Woody dove to the floor and rolled under the table while pulling his AK into shooting position.

Rourke stepped into the hallway; leaving the left gun on full auto, he focused on the table under which Woody the Wood Pecker was trying to fire from. Rourke had dealt immediate death to the first four; they were now on permanent coffee break. His left handed MP-7 demolished the top of the kitchen table and stitched Woody to the floor. Woody had never gotten a shot off; pulling his trigger repeatedly accomplished nothing. His bolt was still locked back.

Rourke swung his right MP-7 to cover the front of the building. Two of the punks came rushing at him from that direction, guns blazing. They rounded the corner into the hall without even looking first to see the threat.

He fired the gun in his right hand out, dropped it to hang from the sling and snatched the CombatMaster from his left arm pit, no need, they were down. He expected to see the two from the roof come charging down the stairwell; freezing for an instant in disbelief at the carnage next to the coffee pot. That would have been all of the time Rourke needed to finish them with the remaining rounds of the MP-7 in his left hand.

They did not appear, *"Good job, Hans"* Rourke thought and drew the .45 riding under his right arm. Rourke did a quick survey of his damage and removed the empty and therefore useless MP-7s. He disengaged the thumb safeties and gripping the two CombatMasters, did an examination of the nine bodies; confirming that none would ever Seig Hail again. Taking a deep breath, he advanced toward the front of the school, toward Sarah and the man that held her hostage.

Since Rourke's first gunshots, he had not been able to hear much. Now in the silence he could hear children and women crying and a man's voice hollering "Was ist das?" over and over. He stepped past the two bodies, careful to avoid the blood leaking out from 9mm holes across their chests and throats and cautiously did a scan around the corner at the end of the hall.

The children had been herded into a corner and the teacher and teacher's assistant were trying to calm them down. Sarah, dressed in an apple-green suit, stood in the center of the room. Behind her was the last terrorist, his pock marked face was flushed and covered in sweat. He was holding a revolver to her head. It looked like a .44 magnum and the hammer stood at full cock—a twitch of the man's trigger finger would be all it took to send a slug tearing through Sarah's skull.

Rourke walked to within ten feet and stopped; then he did something illogical. He reholstered his .45s and snapped the retaining straps back in place. Slowly pulling a folding metal chair up, Rourke straddled it and sat down resting his arms on the chair back.

"Was ist das?" The terrorist asked.

Rourke said, "Look. I don't speak German, do you speak English?" The man nodded. "Excellent, here's where we are. Police and special weapons teams will be here inside of..." Rourke checked his watch and continued," ...a little less than three minutes. Do you understand?"

"Dah, I understand."

"Good, when they get here, they are going to pump tear gas into this building, come charging in and people, including you are going to die. In fact, especially you are going to die. I can keep that from happening and we can all walk outta here. Let the hostages go, please."

"Nein, nein. That I will not do."

"Okay, I thought as much but figured I would try anyway. Tell you what, I'm going to stand up and move this chair and walk out. If you change your mind before I leave the building I can save your life. The rest of your men are dead, wanna see? They are right down that hallway, all dead." Rourke temporarily locked eyes with Sarah and with two quick flicks of his eyes directed her to her left. Her slight nod was his only hope she really understood.

Rourke rose from the chair, pointed with his left hand and slightly turned as he drew the Colt Python from its holster in the small of his back, then he kicked the metal folding chair across the room. The terrorist had glanced toward the hallway, hoping to see one of his men and he jerked at the sound of the chair, pulling the revolver from Sarah's head, pointing it at Rourke.

That's the instant Rourke fired, twice. Rourke had thumb cocked the hammer as he drew the Colt and was counting on the buttery smooth Python double action for two quick controlled shots. The first 158 grain jacketed hollow point crashed into the man's elbow, destroying the ulnar nerve of the neo-Nazi's gun arm and preventing a spasm that would have caused the weapon to discharge;

the second .357 round slammed him high in the right shoulder spinning him away from Sarah as she leaned left and collapsed to her knees. The .44 revolver was slung across the room by the combined momentums of actions.

Five minutes later, the front door of the school opened; with the remaining terrorist in the lead wearing Rourke's discarded tie as a tourniquet. This staunched the blood pouring from "Pocked Mark's" mangled elbow; the gunshot wound in his shoulder needed medical care. Rourke prodded him with one of the Detonics .45s while Rourke's other arm was protectively around Sarah's waist. They walked out followed by a "herd" of children, their teacher and an assistant teacher.

Wolfgang Mann and a squad of Security Police rushed forward. Sarah kissed Rourke on the cheek and ran to Mann. Two of the Security Police grabbed, quickly searched the terrorist and cuffed him, careful to avoid the stink of bodily fluids and excrement that resulted when the terrorist punk had faced death and his bladder and bowels had opened. The others charged the building.

Rourke saw Emma coming through the barricades wearing his suit coat. She came up and kissed him hard on the lips, then leaned back and asked, "Are ya looking for these, Cowboy?" He took the cigar case, opened it, lit one with the Zippo and after inhaling deeply said, "Yes, Ma'am I surely was."

The President of New Germany, now with his arm around Sarah's waist came up on Rourke. They shook hands formally then embraced and Mann whispered, "How can I thank you John?"

Rourke stepped back and seriously said, "How about taking better care of our girl, Wolfgang." Then he smiled and laughed. "Look, these guys were tough when it was ten men against Sarah. Luckily, they were amateurs that had delusions of grandeur. Sarah could have taken them herself if she hadn't been caught off guard. Your protection detail was caught completely off guard, they never had a chance. These punks were really good at executions but with someone shooting at them; they weren't that tough. We were damned lucky."

Mann said, "Thank you my friend." Putting his arm around Sarah, he led her off. Turning to Emma, Rourke said, "We have to go shopping, these dress pants have had it." Looking down at torn, grimy blood soaked pants; she shook her head and then nodded.

Sergeant Hans Jäger cut through the crowd with his sniper weapon slung over one shoulder. "Herr Generaloberst..." Rourke cut him off. "Damn it Hans, what did I tell you?" Jäger looked quickly down and then looked up with an embarrassed smile, "You're right, I'm sorry John." Rourke grinned, "That's better my friend. I don't know about you but I'm about ready for a cold beer." Jäger smiled, "So am I John, I'm buying."

Chapter Six

Emma had gone to the hospital with Sarah, outside of some scratches and contusions and the memories involved with her hostage situation and the execution of her protection detail; she was uninjured. Emma knew those memories would haunt Sarah forever.

Later, Rourke and Wolfgang sat in Mann's office alone and silent. Rourke broke the silence with a slap on the coffee table that separated them. Mann jumped in startled response, "Okay, Wolf here is my position. Your security man was correct; his job was to protect you. However, your job was to protect Sarah. Your so-called security team got themselves executed in front of my ex-wife. She was taken hostage and had to witness that, as well as being abused by a crew of idiots. You let another man save your wife; I don't understand that and never will. I should have and would have died trying to rescue her had a single member of that conglomeration of fools actually been a trained and dedicated soldier. They weren't, that is the only reason Sarah and I are alive right now. You and I have fought together; you and I have fought each other. You are better than this, this should never have happened, but it did. I want to know how and why it happened."

Wolfgang Mann, the leader of New Germany sat dejected and dispirited. Finally, he sat down his cocktail, stood up and started pacing. When he turned, Rourke saw a man at the end of his ropes. "Yes, John, I was a fighter and a good one but the last shot I fired in anger was twelve years ago. I have pulled my country together and now we are one of the two most secure and productive countries on the face of the earth; yours being the other. John, now I am a leader not a fighter. I am responsible for everything that happens in this country. You're correct, today has shown me I have turned into a politician not a leader. I have underestimated a faction that can and will destroy my country and very nearly killed my wife which would have destroyed my life. I cannot give you an excuse for this and I will not bother to offer an explanation for something not worthy of an explanation. I can tell you this, I understand. I get it and tomorrow there will be significant and wide sweeping changes not just in what we are doing but how we are doing it. I am angry; angry at these fools that almost killed my wife and could have killed you. I'm angry at my advisors who convinced me that moderation and compromise was the answer, but mostly I am angry at myself for allowing the opportunity of this to ever occur."

Rourke stood up and extended his hand, "Wolfgang, I only ask one thing of you. Protect the mother of my children and grandmother of my grandchildren." Mann withdrew from the handshake and turned to the window of his office. Rourke started to exit the office but was stopped when Mann said, "John, thank you."

Rourke turned toward his past enemy, current friend and husband-in-law and nodded once and said, "Wolfgang my life has taught me that our enemies never go away, they are always present and always a threat. We can never let our guard down. One of America's first Presidents said, 'The price of freedom is eternal vigilance.' I heard another one I think you ought to remember. It was attributed to Sir Lancelot and it goes, 'It is peace not war that destroys men; it is comfort not danger that breeds cowardice; it is plenty not need that breeds greed and avarice.'" Then Rourke quietly closed the door behind himself.

Two days later, the ceremony to dedicate the new Dr. John Thomas Rourke Medical College went off without a hitch. Wolf and Sarah Rourke-Mann hosted the ceremony and celebration. After Rourke cut the silk ribbon and declared the facility "open for business" he and Emma joined the New Germany Head of State and First Lady for a social gathering. Sarah had not seen Rourke since her rescue. During cocktails she excused herself and strolled over to Emma and John. Emma greeted her with a curtsy and said, "Madam First Lady you look beautiful" then she winked. Sarah smiled and winked back and with a grin said, "Madam Mrs. Doctor General you are exquisite." Then they hugged. "Emma, may I speak to John for a moment?"

"I was just going to refresh our drinks, can I get you anything?" Sarah shook her head, "Thanks anyway, I'm good." Emma nodded and left the two standing with some degree of privacy.

"How are you feeling Sarah?"

"Better John, not good but better. Physically I'm fine; nerves are still a little ragged. I want to thank you again for rescuing me."

"My privilege," was all Rourke could think of to say. Sarah also was at a loss for words so she just kissed him and turned back to see Wolfgang watching them; he smiled and held up his cocktail in salute. Rourke returned the gesture, "Sarah, wait." She turned at look at him, a question in her eyes.

"Tell Wolf I complement him on his security tonight, much better."

"I will John; he'll appreciate that coming from you. Good night and have a safe trip; when do you leave?"

"Day after tomorrow; I love you Sarah."

"I love you too, be safe. Give Emma my thanks." With that she turned and as much as would ever be possible stepped out of his life and back into hers, until the next time...

Chapter Seven

John Rourke rolled backward off the gunwale, Emma splashing in a moment after, three of the SEALs already in the water, along with the archeological dive team; the rest of the SEAL Team on and around the small armada at the dive site. Rourke and his wife had spent several hours a day for the previous ten days mastering the latest version of the by-now primitive hemo-sponges and "wings" with which Rourke had first become familiar at Mid-Wake so long ago. The latest gear better controlled oxygen, better controlled pressure and, in short, made working at what would have been hardhat depths in the 20th Century as easy as going for a swim—so long as one protected the integrity of the suit. It could best be described as a "space suit" for undersea exploration.

Rourke rolled and treaded water just below the surface as he gave himself a final check. Rather than his own weapons—with which he felt considerably more at ease—both he and Emma wore latest SEAL Team issue, which translated to the latest in weaponry as designed and produced by Lancer. Lancer had started out as a sort of boutique weapons company, making unbelievably faithful duplicates of some of the more popular and more advanced handguns of the very late 20th Century, fabricating these for customers with an abundance of cash and good taste. Rourke had taken a liking to the people and their project, not only happy to see some of his favorite weapons return to the marketplace, but always so much of a supporter of capitalism that, in other days, as he might drive past a child's lemonade stand, he'd always hold the good thought that it would succeed.

Lancer executives had, after virtually signing their names in blood, talked Rourke into allowing his own personal weapons—one at a time—to leave his care long enough to be faithfully copied. That was why, the discriminating shooter or collector—were both in abundance these days. Firearms ownership and carry conceal permits were officially encouraged by many of the world's governments—the ones that were to be trusted.

On Rourke's equipment belt was the latest in the Lancer pistol line, cosmetically based on the SIG pistols but loaded with electronics. All Rourke knew of the pistol was that it looked and felt like a SIG 226, one of the pistols of choice of the original SEALs before the Night Of The War fired "smart rounds" and made no noise other than mechanical. When needed, a slide lock could be activated, to eliminate even that. On Rourke's left side was his latest knife, a strong spear point design with a five and half inch blade, the primary cutting edge being augmented by double edged portion that extended three inches along the spine, with an inch and a half of serrations. It was one of two special designs he had commissioned for everyday use. Both were high-carbon tool steel and the Micarta handles came off with an Allen wrench to allow proper cleaning and care. In its current "dive knife" configuration, it was imperative to remove the salt water from the knife and its Kydex holster before it went back into the normal leather sheath.

Emma nodded that her last gear check was finished and Rourke gestured toward her with his right hand, waving her ahead of him as they followed the dive rope toward the sandy bottom.

Navy SEALs were admittedly an unusual accompaniment for an archeological expedition; but, after the contents of the first wine and olive oil jars brought to the surface were even cursorily examined, security of the highest order was immediately put into play.

Off the coast of what had once—centuries before—been Egypt, as natural global cooling had progressed, helped by the nuclear winter in the aftermath of The Night of the War, sea levels dropped. Rourke's briefing on the jars had included reminders that, had sea levels risen or even remained the same, the vessel and its contents might never have been discovered, the treasure contained there lost as it had been since 48BC, when Julius Caesar—either by design or by chance—had burned the Library of Alexandria, the greatest repository of knowledge in the ancient world. Rourke had always hoped the library had not been put to the torch, but that the library had become part of the conflagration during the resultant fire storm. Some estimates put the number of books lost at around forty thousand, each of these taking up several Papyrus scrolls, originals of some of the works great literature and others shrouded in the mystery of time. Apparently, as the wine and olive oil jars suggested, someone with a passion for the contents of the library sought to safeguard as many works as he could, either saving them from the flames or sending off originals or copies in the fire's aftermath, as a hedge against future loss.

Emma followed the rope downward, pennants marking depth attached to the rope. One other item John Rourke had left topside was his Rolex, good to a ridiculous depth to be sure, but the SEAL issue chronometer's digital readout was easier to see and the unit's additional functions potentially useful.

Below, barely visible through the gently swirling clouds of sand, Rourke made out the vague outline of a ship's hull. Ever so slightly, Rourke quickened his rate of descent.

As one of only six living people who had survived The Night of The War to live in the present day, John Thomas Rourke was always being contacted for one thing or another. Responding to these requests for his time or insight kept him busy, at times busier than he liked. The formula for Coca-Cola had at last been cracked and the legendary beverage could once again be available. He tried it. Paul tried it. Natalia tried it. Sarah flew in from New Germany and tried it. The would-be entrepreneurs went back to their chemistry labs to substantially tweak the formula. Somehow, John Rourke and those members of "The Family" who had been adults before the Night of The War, where considered "experts" on the past.

When the invitation to join the marine archeological unit had arrived, it was from the Chief of Naval Operations, addressed to "Doctor General John Thomas Rourke." Rourke wouldn't have refused if he thought he could.

Emma stopped a few feet above the wrecked vessel's remains, swimming effortlessly from port to starboard over the ship, forward to aft, the gracefulness of her movements reminding Rourke of a butterfly, flying almost languorously over a garden.

The contents of the jars first brought to the surface by the archeological team, some scrolls in a language totally unknown, were obviously rescued from the destruction of the World's Library.

"John." Emma's voice came to him as clearly as if she were whispering beside him.

"What, sweetheart?"

"These years we've been married; being your wife has let me see and do some cool stuff. But, this has got to be the coolest, John. I mean, history we never even knew existed is going to be unfolding before our eyes. Civilizations we never..."

"Don't get carried away. Okay, we've found a language no one can read. I'm sure we'll find some more enigmas. So far, this has significant potential; but, we don't know if it's Earth-shattering."

"Aren't you enthused?"

"Yes, I am, Emma—only I'm five hundred years older, technically, so that may tend to weigh on my enthusiasm." Actually, he was just as excited as she. It was like finding and opening a novel written by one's favorite author, a novel never known to exist. What was inside could be magnificent—or, perhaps, disappointing.

Rourke joined his wife over the ship, the archeological team using things like great vacuum cleaners to move aside the sediment and reveal the presence of more jars. Some, of course, lamentably, were shattered, their contents destroyed. Could the bits and pieces of that jar or that one have held within it the cure for cancer—albeit cancer was inoculated against these days and, what few cancers that did manifest themselves were easily cured. The "cure for cancer" was a 20th Century man's way of describing a longed for medical miracle. *The cure for the common cold—that was it*, Rourke thought, smiling. Although most rhinoviruses were easily treatable these days, there was no actual "cure."

Rourke and Emma moved closer to the archeological party. Several more jars were being freed and jars uncovered from the sediment earlier were carefully cocooned within padded nets and were being hoisted to the surface, to go aboard the "Desperado," where they would be carefully opened under controlled conditions of temperature and humidity and subjected to initial examination. Rourke, Emma following him, slowly swam over the wreckage site, then started to the surface, going quite slowly as an added—and essentially unnecessary— precaution.

There was very little marine life, the ongoing activity at the archeological site discouraging all but the occasional school of fish whose size would have made them eligible for the dubious honor of being designated "sardines."

"Are we still going to stay around for a few days?" Emma asked.

Rourke glanced below him along the rope they followed for the ascent. "I was thinking we would. Work for you?"

"You know I'd ..."

Emma's voice cut off. Rourke was still looking at her. Nothing seemed different. He looked up. One of the SEALS who rotated through guarding the operation from the water was floating dead, his suit torn open in a long gash, his intestines hanging out. There would be an entrance wound in the back, Rourke thought clinically as he drew the Lancer smart pistol. He saw a dark figure moving through the water, wearing a type of environment suit different from anything Rourke had ever seen, what had to be a weapon attached to the wearer's right wrist. One of the SEALs was interposing himself between Emma and the strangely attired armed figure. The SEAL fired and Rourke could see the smart rounds literally bouncing off the environment suit. Emma fired, her "bullets" doing the same. There were several men in the strange environment suits, Rourke realized some swimming toward the Desperado itself.

The man who'd likely killed the first SEAL aimed his wrist and the device attached to it at the second SEAL, the SEAL going for their attacker with his knife, but too far away before another shot could be fired. Rourke was already in motion, ordering his wife, "Get close to me. We've got to go topside," as he body slammed the man in the environment suit in the split second after the attacker shot the second SEAL. Rourke had the issue knife in his right hand, the smart weapon on his right hip useless against whoever the attackers were. As the attacker turned the weapon strapped to his wrist toward Emma, Rourke was on him. Somehow, because of the strange environment suit, the smart bullets bouncing off it and the energy weapon on its wrist, Rourke had expected something more than a man.

It was a man. Rourke's knife blade skittered off the environment suit, Rourke feeling the energy emanating from the suit. What had stopped smart bullets was working against Rourke's knife. Rourke shifted the knife to his left

47

hand, grabbing the smart pistol from his holster. Rourke didn't waste time trying to fire it. He turned it in his hand and beat at where the face would have to be within the environment suit. Each blow Rourke hammered made Rourke's hand and arm almost going numb, the energy shield doing its work. Rourke kept at it, his eyes scanning the environment suit as his enemy was bringing the energy weapon up.

The energy weapon was about to fire point blank, Rourke dropped the useless smart pistol and shoved the energy weapon and the wrist to which it was attached left and away from Rourke's body plane. As he did so, the weapon fired. But, John Rourke had planned ahead, realizing that the energy field would need to be timed to the shots from the wrist device, in order to keep the energy pulse from shattering the very bones to which it was attached. Rourke stabbed the knife into the attacker's right forearm and drew the knife's tip upward, cutting along the suit, through the flesh beneath it, along the upper arm, across the shoulder and the right clavicle, into the carotid artery.

Rourke pushed the dead man off the knife, glanced toward where he hoped Emma would be and found her there. "We have to get to the conventional weapons we have on board the Desperado." Easier said than done, John Rourke reminded himself. He gestured away from the guide rope and, after glancing about them, found one of the quadrants surrounding the Desperado that seemed devoid of any of the attackers in the strange environment suits. Emma followed him; Rourke's swim roughly following the mid-line of the Desperado's hull.

Aft was as good a place as any to board the Desperado, Rourke dodging the vessel's twin screws. Another dead body, then another and still another floated past, only to crash into one another or bounce off the stern. Timing would be everything. He glanced at Emma, her knife in her right hand. Rourke needed a better knife, as well as real guns. Once free of the water, Rourke's and Emma's own environment suits would need to be breached within a few minutes at most, any longer than that potentially damaging to the lungs.

The knife clenched in his right fist, Rourke broke surface, glancing quickly to right and left, finding the stern ladder and starting up. He reached the top of the ladder, surveying the scene on the main deck of the Desperado. Far forward, there was some actual hand-hand-fighting, the surviving SEALs apparently choosing to fight-on despite the fact their pistols and submachine guns were useless against this enemy. Rourke noticed, too, that the attackers could apparently wear their environment suits in the water or out, a technology well in advance of anything Rourke knew to exist.

Rourke flipped the rail, his lungs already starting to tell him he had to breach his suit. As Emma came over the rail, Rourke tore the hood and hemo-sponge regulator away. Rourke's wife did the same. In a low crouch, his knife in a rapier hold, Rourke edged away from the rail. They might have only seconds. A Navy SEAL was locked in mortal combat with one of the attackers. Rourke grabbed the man's face with his left hand, feeling the suit's force field pushing his hand away. Rourke held on, the knife in his right hand pushing and pushing toward the enemy's throat, the young SEAL broke free. The SEAL took his knife and stabbed at the attacker's right arm as the arm and the weapon on the wrist came into line with the SEAL's body.

Rourke gave up on slitting his enemy's throat. The force shield was too much. But, with all the strength he could summon to his right arm, Rourke stabbed the double edged SEAL knife toward where the Adam's apple should be, hoping the blade would not be deflected by the field. Rourke felt contact, penetrating the environment suit and the throat within it. Rourke ripped the knife right, cautioning the SEAL, "Watch for the blood spray, son. Not quite sure what we're fighting," Rourke added as he let the body drop. Rourke half-vaulted down into the companionway, hoping Emma was right behind him. He started forward, toward the cabin they shared, kicked open the door—his key was with his regular clothes, topside.

There was a small closet in the cabin. "Emma," Rourke rasped.

"Right behind you."

"Arm up, Emma."

There was a large leather bag in the bottom, zippered shut and closed with a combination lock. Rourke spun the combination, unzipped and took a double Alessi shoulder rig from inside, slipping it over his shoulders. The twin stainless Detonics CombatMaster .45s were in pouches built into the bag. There was no time to check the pistols. They'd been chamber loaded when he left them and there had been no sign of tampering. There was a wide Milt Sparks belt, two Milt Sparks Six-Packs—everything a Lancer copy—on the belt, for twelve spare magazines in all. Rourke closed the belt around his waist.

Emma's taste in ordnance was her own, eclectic to say the least. From Lancer's archives, years earlier, when the children were younger, she'd chosen a brace of Third Generation Smith & Wesson autos, actually seeing their magazine safeties as a plus with kids around. They were 5906s, fifteen plus one capacity, all stainless steel, weighing two pounds thirteen ounces loaded with 115-grain Jacketed Hollow Points. For that reason, her gun belt was only set up for one pistol and a Milt Sparks Six-Pack. As she buckled the cross draw holstered Smith to her waist, he noticed her taking the second pistol from her case and shoving it under her belt.

Rourke reached into the closet and took the long, zippered case. Before The Night of The War, his friends at Century International Arms had told them of their plans to produce an all-American made AK-47, with a receiver machined from eleven pounds of 4140 ordnance steel. Things went so quickly in those last months; the world situation growing worse and worse, Rourke never knew if the gun was ever produced. Thinking it a magnificent idea, Rourke had shared every detail he could remember of that conversation with the designers at Lancer and inside the case was Lancer's latest rifle, the Century Arms Centurion 39, all USA made semi-automatic only 7.62X39mm AK-47.

Rourke pulled the rifle from the case and extracted three thirty-round magazines from outside pouches. These he stuffed into a mussete bag from the leather case. Slinging the mussete bag cross-body, Rourke was out the cabin door, Emma behind. He estimated they'd spent about forty seconds arming up. A lot of people could have been killed in forty seconds.

Rourke started the magazine into the Centurion 39, the lip catching. Rourke rocked it back into the seated position.

Emma right behind him, Rourke started up the companionway steps.

One of the attackers, still fully clad in his environment suit, was on the way down. The man raised his wrist and fired his energy weapon, blowing out a hole in the bulkhead not far from Rourke's head. Rourke noted, "You missed; I won't," holding the Centurion 39 to his shoulder. He fired once, the enemy's body going rigid as the 123-grain Full Metal Case bullet—thank God, Rourke thought—penetrated the energy field around the environment suit, into the chest. Rourke fired again, putting the second round into the attacker's head. "That's reassuring," Rourke smiled.

Cautiously, but quickly, Rourke stepped up onto the main deck, reminding Emma, "Stay close and fire double taps with that 9mm of yours."

"Gotcha," she answered.

Rourke suddenly thought of the gorgeous combat pilot he'd met years ago, falling in love with her in spite of himself; and, a different sort of smile crossed his lips.

Rourke searched for a bad guy, found one just starting to aim his wrist mounted energy weapon. Rourke snatched the Detonics CombatMaster from under his left arm, thumbed back the hammer and fired at the attacker's head. The body went rigid, staggered a moment, and then collapsed. So far, so good.

It was late afternoon, long shadows on the main deck as outnumbered SEALs, whose weapons were essentially useless, fought unrelentingly against their attackers. Rourke handed off the Centurion 39 to the SEAL Team Commander, handing him the mussete bag with the spare magazines, as well. "Don't lose it; I like it. It's semi-auto only and rounds penetrate the suit. One or two per bad guy should be all it takes."

"Thank you, sir!"

Rourke handed Emma the CombatMaster from his left hand. "Let me borrow one of your 5906s. It's an experiment," Rourke advised.

She handed him the pistol from her belt. Rourke was already hearing well-spaced, single shots from the Centurion 39.

Rourke found another target, unable to go for a full-frontal shot. He fired the Smith & Wesson, a double tap to the throat of the attacker. The man spun right, turning toward them, then spiraled to the deck.

Rourke told his wife, "Find two lucky SEALs, loan them your pistols and split your spare magazines between them. Advise double taps. You keep my Detonics and I'll supply the magazines."

Rourke drew the second CombatMaster from beneath his right arm, shifting the .45 to his right hand. After a moment, Emma was back beside him and Rourke started forward, clearing the main deck. Rourke had no idea of the fight's duration thus far, but from that moment onward, everything was done in under a minute. A half dozen of the attackers getting away, at least a dozen more dead on the main deck or elsewhere were aboard the Desperado. The SEAL Team leader, a Lieutenant Torquelson, made to return Rourke's rifle. Rourke advised, "Keep the weapon for a while longer. You'll need to make sure no enemy personnel are lurking aboard the other vessels, or still in the water, waiting to strike. You'll want to check for explosives, electronic eaves-dropping gear and the like. We'll check the Desperado."

Some of the marine archeological personnel were coming up onto the main deck, some of them armed, but with smart weapons only. They, of course, were useless. Rourke was reminded of the great lack of success the model 1894 .38 Colt had experienced against the Moro tribesmen during the Philippine Insurrection. History was repeating itself, it seemed.

Emma organized parties of archeological personnel to carefully check every inch of the vessel, while Rourke sat down on a tool box beside the body of the man he'd shot with Emma's 9mm. Rourke began examining the portion of the suit which covered the attacker's head. There was no access seam. The first way into the suit that he found was along the left rib cage, from just below the armpit to the pelvis. Rourke opened the suit, finding naked flesh—a little pale seeming, but otherwise normal—beneath.

It was several minutes before Emma re-joined Rourke. He had, only a moment earlier, gotten through the portion of the suit which covered the face. Rourke sat there staring at it. Emma dropped to her knees on the deck.

After a long seeming silence, John Rourke spoke. "Emma? Remember my speaking about the Eden Project's return?"

"You kind of skimmed over some of the more dangerous parts—at least the way Paul tells it."

"That's not what I mean. Remember my mentioning Captain Dodd, the Eden Project Commander?"

"He went bad, afterward—right?"

"He did. Ever wonder what he looked like?"

"I can't say that I have," Emma admitted.

"Well, if you ever do, just look at the photos we'll have of this guy's face. Right down to the almost triangular shaped mole on his left earlobe."

"What are you saying, John?"

"I'm saying you're looking at a perfect clone of Captain Dodd, wearing an environment suit, electronically shielded, a man who's been dead for centuries, whom I just shot before he could use his energy weapon. The suit, the shield, the weapon—all beyond our technology, unless the military is suddenly holding back from me; we have a problem." Finding the closure mechanism for the environmental suit, Rourke carefully exposed the torso of Captain Dodd. There was a tattoo on the left side of Dodd's chest between the collarbone and nipple; Rourke frowned. He had seen that image before, a long, long time ago. Turning toward the bow of the boat where the SEAL had gathered, Rourke shouted "Lieutenant Torquelson, come here please."

At the double quick Torquelson responded, "Aye Sir?"

"Lieutenant, I want the body and any others in these environmental suits you have located secured immediately. I want them placed in body bags with every scrap of material, equipment, anything associated with them; arrange to have them refrigerated. I need you to contact Mid-Wake and get a military transport here—and I mean yesterday. The transport is to take them back to Mid-Wake for examination. I want you to place your team and every survivor from this event in immediate lock-down isolation until they have been debriefed at Mid-Wake, me included. I want zero media coverage of this event—zero. I am declaring a Delta Red Condition. Do you understand my orders?"

Squatting down, Torquelson whispered, "Sir, yes Sir. Do we have a biohazard situation?"

"No, something much worse. I also want you to contact my son and have him standing by to meet the transport when we arrive. Have you got a digital camera?"

Torquelson nodded and over his shoulder shouted, "Sparks, bring the camera, now."

Seaman Sparks jumped to and presented the camera to the Lieutenant, "Here Sir."

Torquelson stood, took the camera, "Stand by Sparks—Smith, I need you over here now, Jamison I want a direct and secure comm. link with Operations at Mid-Wake. We are now in a Delta Red Condition. I want this area secured immediately; I want two men in the water with a third on over watch ready to respond. Let's jump to it people."

Rourke took the camera and snapped several shots of Dodd from different angles, finally reopening the environmental suit and snapped several pictures of Dodd's chest before handing the camera back to Torquelson. "I want this camera placed inside three separately sealed plastic bags and secured in the strongest water proof transport container you have."

"Understood Sir, I take it this is important."

"Lieutenant, you are hereby relieved of your duties within the team; have your second-in-command take over and finish preparations for our removal from this area. You are, as of now, personally responsible for insuring this camera is delivered to Mid-Wake. If none of us and nothing makes it to Mid-Wake, that camera has to. I want a radio beacon attached to the case, so that if the plane goes down it can be found. You will personally insure when the photos are seen, my son, Michael is in the room. Are there any questions?"

"Dr. Rourke, I have a bunch of questions but I suspect they are ones you're not going to answer. Am I correct?"

"You are Lieutenant and I'm sorry. You're going to have to trust me on this. I want that transport here as soon as it can be. Contact the archeology team and tell them this site is closed and is now considered a National Security Area."

Several hours later a Mid-Wake Airboat transport landed off the port bow and anchored. The Desperado moved into position to transfer the wounded, the dead, the survivors and the camera.

Chapter Eight

Paula Rourke plopped down on the bed. Amanda's far wall was the room's computer screen and, as Paula watched, streams of numbers ran across the entire wall. "This is old computer code stuff," Amanda told her. "I just thought you might like to see a little. All of the original computer stuff for the Eden Project? That's how it was."

"Holy crap," Paula murmured softly. Amanda Jones was a year plus her senior, just turned seventeen and already attending classes at Mid-Wake University, home to Hawaii for only a few days, her mother—born with a congenital problem—finally relenting to an artificial heart transplant—it was that or death. It was routine surgery, but Amanda's mother disliked any sort of medical procedure, which was why Amanda was an only child. After Amanda had been born, the OB/GYN had advised Amanda's mother that any future deliveries would have to be Caesarian. This was also the reason Amanda spent only half her time living with her mother and the other half with her father, who lived at Mid-Wake, a Naval Commander.

Amanda's mother, Paula thought, was likely the reason why Amanda was sort of the ultimate computer person. She could even build her own computer. But, her genius—everyone admitted it, took it for granted—was in her ability to bring what amounted to a "sixth sense" to data decryption, no matter how obscure.

As a fourth grade science project—Paula, in third grade at the time, had built a working model of a volcano. At about the same time, Amanda had begun decrypting the computer logs of the Eden Project on its approximately five hundred year voyage in an elliptical orbit which took it far, far away from earth—no one really knew exactly how far and flung the vessels back to return to Earth five centuries after The Night of The War, when humanity had nearly been obliterated.

Unlike a lot of girls her age, Paula took history very seriously. After all, her father, John Rourke, had not only been there to observe history, but had literally saved humanity. He was the greatest hero in the history of all mankind.

Without his efforts, life on Earth and below the Sea would be totally different, if there were any life at all.

After becoming fast friends, Paula and Amanda had a pact. Amanda would decrypt history and Paula would translate it into prose which people could read and study, stories at which mankind could marvel. Her uncle/brother-in-law Paul Rubenstein, perhaps the most famous writer on the planet, had been helping her with things like style and all the other things writers had to know. Uncle Paul was a great guy, Uncle Paul and Aunt Annie (her half-sister) two of her most favorite people ever.

The concierge's voice interrupted Paula's thoughts. "Would either of you girls care for some refreshments?"

"What have you got?" Amanda asked the disembodied voice.

"As to liquid refreshments available to young ladies your ages, we have six different types of soda, including two colas. I can have the kitchen make pizza, if you girls would like."

Amanda stood up and walked to the center of the room, Paula joining her. "Pizza sounds good," Paula remarked.

"Pepperoni pizza and a water and..." Amanda looked at Paula.

"Root beer, concierge, if you've got it."

"The refreshments you ladies have ordered will be ready shortly. I will alert you when they are." The voice of the concierge was gone. Amanda was staring at the vanity wall. Paula stood beside her. The vanity wall—not every home had one, but Amanda's step father—whom she really didn't like—was always trying to win her over with luxury. There was a vanity wall at Paula's house, but everyone kept paying her father to make speeches and dedicate things and this huge military pension—he'd been made a general—had accumulated for him while he was in cryogenic sleep. Her mom and dad had more money than they could ever possibly spend.

As Paula looked at the wall, Amanda ordered it, "Left profile." The field of view changed their image in the vanity wall shown from their left side. "Full face close," Amanda directed it. Their faces were filling the screen that was the wall. Amanda's chocolate brown skin was spotless, her brown eyes beautiful, her black hair short and kinky. Paula had read the term "afro" and Amanda, always a little retro fashion-wise, was fighting a one girl crusade for the style to return. So far, the crusade wasn't working. Amanda was the only black girl Paula knew who wore her hair that way.

Paula looked at herself. At almost sixteen, her face had lost most of its youthful chubbiness. She had her father's brown eyes and brown hair, wearing her hair past her shoulders, as her mother did. Her mother's auburn hair was really beautiful, unlike her own. Her father—because of, to a large degree, the cryogenic sleeps John Rourke had taken—despite the date when he was born back in the 20th Century, looked to be an extremely vigorous forty or so. She had heard him described that way so often by so many people that she never questioned it.

Amanda interrupted her thoughts. "Now, you can't breathe a word of this until I've written the paper on it, Paula. Swear."

"I swear."

"In the Eden Project's computer logs, I found an anomaly. There's a period of almost three Earth years while the entire fleet is in some sort of 'geo-synchronous' orbit around some large object that's not large enough to be a planet or even a good-sized moon. And then, the whole Eden Project Fleet is back on its way again."

"What happened in those three years?" Paula said, sitting down on the edge of the bed again, pulling her legs up under her skirt.

"I don't know yet, and I'll never mine all the data I need to tell anything for sure; but, I've discovered I can track movements between the individual ships in the Fleet and whatever they were orbiting around for three years. And, I can maybe find more."

"What would it mean?" Paula asked her friend.

"I'm just guessing. But, I think they were waylaid—and boarded."

Paula sucked in her breath.

The voice of the concierge alerted them, "The pepperoni pizza and the beverages are now available. I'm afraid there's no staff member available to serve you young ladies."

"That's okay, concierge. We'll get it ourselves," Amanda responded. The apartment was fully automated and the bedroom door opened as Paula and Amanda approached it; the two girls ate ravenously.

Michael, her uncle and half-brother, picked Paula up at eleven, as promised. Paula could never get over how good looking he was, like a younger version of her father, but different, somehow. "Get in, kid," Michael told her, the gull wing door of his sports car rose up. Paula slipped into the front seat, the door lowering, her seat restraints securing around her. "So, you and Amanda have fun?"

"Yeah. She told me something I can't tell you or anyone. I promised, you know?" Paula looked at Michael and he nodded.

"Is she in some kind of trouble?"

"No, Uncle Michael, nothing like that. It's just some historical discovery she may made." Even though Michael was actually her half-brother, Paula enjoyed picking on him with her pet name for him, "Makes you seem older and wiser than a brother," she had told him

"Well, I've never heard of anyone getting hurt by history. Not knowing history can hurt you a lot. But, knowledge is power."

"Golly, Uncle Michael! Can I write that down so I don't forget it? 'Knowledge is power.' Wow."

"You're a smart ass." Swatting her on the knee he heard the beep on his comm. link. Pulling the device from his pocket he hit the icon to get the message. He read it once, frowned and pulled off the highway onto the shoulder and read it again. He hit the call link when the line was opened. He said, "This is Michael Rourke, message received and acknowledged. Do we have any details?" He listened for several minutes before speaking, finally saying, "Is there an ETA?" The answer came but only Michael could hear it. Paula was beginning to frown, "What's wrong?" Michael waved her to hush, Paula frowned deeper but stopped asking questions.

"That's affirmative, I'll be there in..." he consulted his wrist watch and made mental calculations. "Give me forty-five minutes," he broke the connection and turned to Paula after making a U-turn and getting back in the flow of traffic now going the opposite direction. "Paula, I need you to call Annie and Paul, I'm going to drop you off with them. There has been some trouble but your mom and dad are alright. They are headed back to Mid-Wake and will be here in about two hours. I'm going to have Natalia meet me at the base."

"What's going on, Uncle Michael?"

"Honey, right now all I know is your mom and dad are okay; others have been injured and they are returning home on an Airboat. I'll have your mom get in touch with you as soon as I can."

Paula nodded and began making her call. Michael contacted Natalia and said simply, "There has been an incident with Dad and Emma, they are okay but are returning to Mid-Wake, arriving in the next couple of hours. I need you to meet me at the base operations building. I'm dropping Paula off at Paul and Annie's. I have her in the car with me now." He wanted Natalia to know he could not speak freely with her sitting there. "I'll call you as soon as I hear something else and I've got the Smart Ass delivered to Annie," he said with an over-the shoulder glance at Paula. She gave a half-smile and continued to talk to Annie; Paula was trying to eaves drop on Michael's conversation as much as talking to Annie.

She broke the connection to Annie and said, "Okay, they know I'm coming and I told them everything that you told me."

"Good, thanks Paula. This probably isn't anything... I just don't know and I don't want you having to hang around the base needlessly when you could be having a good supper and watching a movie."

"Uncle Michael, you are a lousy liar, but I appreciate it. Let me know something as soon as you can and have Mom give me a call so I know they are really okay."

"I will Honey, I promise." Then he squeezed another ten miles an hour out of the car's speed.

Chapter Nine

Michael was half-way across the parking lot headed to the Operations Building when Natalia drove up. She slid to a stop next to his car and hurried over to him, her high-heels clicked on the pavement. "What do we know?" were her first words.

"Not much more than I told you initially," he gave her a quick kiss and they started walking. "There was some kind of an attack force at the ship wreck site. After an underwater incursion in which some SEALs were killed, Dad and Emma were able to get to the Desperado and get their weapons. The bad guys had some kind of environmental suit that the SEAL weaponry was useless against. A couple, don't know how many were killed; others were injured or wounded, again don't know how many. At least one of the opposing forces was killed and Dad called Delta Red Condition and ordered an immediate evacuation back to Mid-Wake. They are in the air now."

"A Delta Red, that is pretty serious. Why a Delta Red?"

"I don't know Natalia, but you know Dad is not one to exaggerate." They flashed their IDs and were escorted to the Operations Building nerve center. A Marine Guard asked again to see their IDs. Once passed him, they were allowed in the Command Post. "Mr. Rourke, I'm Commander Johnson. I got the duty on this one."

"Pleasure Commander, this is my wife Natalia."

"Ma'am," Johnson turned back to Michael. "Mr. Rourke, as you know with a Delta Red Condition normal communication is highly restricted. Therefore, there is not a lot more information I can tell you at this time. The Airboat is on final approach, about 45 minutes out. We have emergency responders and equipment, medical personnel, military intelligence and investigators on site and ready to respond. We can do nothing more at this moment. Do you have any questions, Sir?"

"No Commander, it sounds like you have it all covered. Now all we can do is wait."

"You're correct Sir, ain't it a bitch."

Michael found the standard Government-issue coffee pot and poured two cups, handing one to Natalia. Taking a sniff she wrinkled her nose, "What is this?" Michael smiled and took a sip, "That Ma'am is what passes for coffee in our military."

Michael was rinsing out their mugs when Commander Johnson waved him to come over to the Comm. Center. "They're about five minutes out, another eight for the descent from the surface and they will be in the hanger. Corporal Daniels here will show you the way."

"We know the way Commander," Natalia said standing.

"Ma'am, we are in a Delta Red Condition. That means this entire center is considered a No Lone Zone. No one, no civilian anyway, is allowed anywhere without an escort, period."

Under Marine escort they descended to the Hanger level. After the final docking sequence had been complete, hatches started popping open both fore and aft. "There they are," Michael said to Natalia pointing. Emma and John tossed a wave and started toward them. Michael spotted a slight limp in his father's gait. Emma and Natalia embraced, John and Michael first grasped hands then did the "guy-back-slap" hug. Michael handed his phone to Emma, "Call Paula, she's with Paul and Annie, I promised."

Emma took the phone with a "Thanks" and dialed the number. Paula answered on the first ring, "Mom, are you guys okay?" As they walked to the debriefing room Emma tried to fend a hundred or more questions while trying to convey that her parents really were healthy and unharmed. Finally Emma said, "Honey, I have to go now but I'll call you as soon as I can. Let me speak to Uncle Paul."

"Emma is everything okay?"

"Paul right now all I can say is John and I are fine, we are back in Mid-Wake. Take care of Paula for us, we'll call you in a couple of hours," then she broke the connection without waiting for an answer and handed the phone back to Michael. The four of them joined Lieutenant Torquelson and the military debriefing team and closed the door behind another Marine guard. As soon as John Thomas Rourke approached the table, Torquelson stood and saluted. "Sir, here is the package," and handed the case with the camera to Rourke. "Thanks

Lieutenant you did a good job. Gentlemen, give me a minute to get this unpacked. Lieutenant, will you explain what occurred?"

A Marine Colonel stood up from the table, "Hold it Dr. Rourke, I am Colonel Donald A. Davenport, the lead member of this debriefing team and the first thing I want to know is how does a civilian have the authority to institute a Delta Red Condition, or for that matter even the knowledge of a Delta Red Condition. I know much about your history Sir and hold you in the highest regard; however, this is a military matter and I'm in charge here."

Rourke waved for the Lieutenant to sit down. Reaching into his back pocket, Rourke retrieved his wallet, thumbed through it for a minute then walked around the table and laid something in front of Colonel Davenport. Rourke knew he had to regain control and do it right now.

"Colonel, I appreciate your regards but not your knowledge of me or my family. If you will notice Sir, this is a military identification card, just like the one you carry. If you will notice also Sir, it lists my rank as General. If you will further notice it carries the signature and seal of the President. That Sir means I am hereby 'pulling rank' on you; now here's how we're going to do this. Lieutenant Torquelson is about to brief you people on what happened. Then I'm going to show you some evidence. At that point you and your people may ask any questions you wish. Is that understood, Colonel?"

The Colonel, after checking Rourke's ID, nodded once and sat down, obviously not enthralled with having been dressed down but smart enough to know when he was outgunned. He flipped the card across the table to Rourke, who calmly smiled, picked it up and (rather enjoying the moment) took his time replacing it in his wallet. Then he turned to Lieutenant Torquelson and said, "LT, you have the floor."

The SEAL Team Commander took a deep breath and began to recite the briefing he had prepared on the flight. Rourke fumbled with the case closures, finally laying the two pieces of the water-proof case on the floor out of the way. Pulling the Sting 1A, he cut the seals of each bag individually and checked each layer of protection for moisture. He laid the intact camera on the table and asked one of the technicians to download the memory card and get the photos ready for display on the main screen.

Torquelson finished his briefing; he saluted and sat back down. John Rourke stood, thanked the SEAL Commander and said, "Were it not for the SEALs under Lieutenant Torquelson's leadership none of the rest of us would be here right now. Here is what we were fighting."

The first several shots were of the Captain Dodd clone with his helmet still on. "This environmental suit was completely impervious to the SEAL weapons. Unless the military has been holding back on me, neither the Russians, the Chinese nor us have this kind of technology. We have a new player in this game." The next shot was of Dodd with the helmet removed.

Michael spoke up, "I know him, that's...." trying to first remember the face and then struggling to find an explanation. "That's Dodd, one of the original Eden Project team, but he's dead."

"Yes, it is Dodd and Dodd is dead, this has to be a clone. There is one more frame you have to see," Rourke nodded to the tech to flash the last frame up on the screen. "This folks is a tattoo I found on Dodd's chest. It took me only a moment to remember the last time I saw this design and it was the only time I've seen this design until now."

The crowd was murmuring trying to decipher the tattoo's significance. Finally, Colonel Davenport stood up, "Doctor General Rourke, are you telling us that you declared a Delta Red Condition because of a tattoo? Sir I find that irresponsible."

Rourke slammed his hands down on the table and said softly and slowly, "Let me tell you something Mister. I have only seen this design one other time in my life and it was back before the Night of the War. I was on a special covert mission inside of what used to be Canada's Arctic Circle. This design was on the belt buckle of a dead pilot whose craft had crashed. It was a craft of unique design and origin whose existence was never publicized. You could even say the craft had an out-of-this world design. It would also be fair to say that the craft and my mission were not ever acknowledged—they were covered up. You might also like to know that the dead pilot was as unique as his craft. In fact, Sir, he was an alien, he was an extra-terrestrial." Rourke paused, never one who favored cursing, he believed it showed a lack of intellect and vocabulary, but in this instance... "He was a God-damn ET."

"I have no idea, zero, as to how this is happening. I have no idea what the connection is between a clone of Captain Dodd and that image. What I can tell you is; once there was a dead alien pilot. I saw his body with my own eyes, I took tissue samples. I took the belt buckle with that image on it and destroyed the craft following a gun battle with the Soviet KGB's top UFO expert, Vassily Batrudinov and Russian Spenatz troops inside the Canadian Arctic Circle. What I can surmise is this; we have a dead clone of a man from the Eden Project. The Eden Project was on a five-hundred year mission in deep space, now the clone of a man from that mission attacks me and my wife off the coast of what used to be Egypt. Lastly, because of that damned tattoo, I believe the security of the world and the human race is in danger and that Colonel, that's why I called the damned Delta Red Condition." The room was silent.

Michael turned to Natalia, her eyes were wide and she shook her head, no. Michael stood up and whispered in John Thomas Rourke's ear, "Dad we have to talk." John nodded.

Chapter Ten

The debriefing took another two hours. John and Emma checked in on Paula and told Paul and Annie as much as they could. Emotionally and physically drained they asked if it was okay for Paula and Timothy, who had been at a friend's home playing video games, to spend the night. Once Paula was assured her parents were okay, she went to help Annie get the evening meal ready. Her job was to heat the olive oil in a large saucepan, mix in 2 cloves garlic, and cook 1 minute. Stir in crushed tomatoes, tomato paste, water, sugar, half the oregano, and bay leaf, season with salt and pepper before bringing to a boil before reducing the heat and letting it simmer. Annie was responsible for the meat balls.

John and Emma returned to their own home and after hitting the hot tub, Emma dabbed some medicinal cream on the scrape on John's left knee cap, a by-product of the fight on the Desperado. They crashed. It was 8:15 the next morning before they were awakened by the doorbell.

Michael and Natalia had brought breakfast. "Dad, I'm sorry to disturb you guys, but... Like I said, we need to talk." John had slipped on jeans to answer the door; he hollered to Emma, "Michael and Natalia are here. They brought breakfast; we'll be on the patio, would you bring some coffee?" A grunt and the rustling of bed clothes served as his answer. When Emma brought the carafe of coffee John was already munching on a croissant.

Michael started his story. "Look, three days ago Natalia and I were summoned for a meeting with President Arthur Hooks and Vice-President Benjamin Richardson. The Presidential security detail apologized to us, but our personal weapons had to be temporarily surrendered."

Natalia spoke up, "I asked Michael, 'If you win the Presidency, will you change that policy?' and he said he would." Rourke smiled and nodded.

"Anyway, we met with the President and the Vice-President. The President felt that, if I run, I'd win, if for no other reason than I'm a Rourke. That said; he felt I needed to be brought up to speed on a few important points."

"Richardson asked," Natalia filled in, 'Perhaps Mrs. Rourke would care to join the President's wife for tea or something.' I had picked up my purse when Michael told the President that I really wasn't all that fond of tea and, if I stayed, it would save him the trouble of remembering every single detail of the conversation which he would have to recount accurately to me. I sat down my purse."

"The President told Natalia and me that there are certain topics the opposition party, the Progressives, will hit me with, to catch me with my pants down, as it were." Natalia smiled and brushed her hand against Michael's arm. "Phillip Greene, the Progressive's obvious candidate, has 'fellow travelers' who've insinuated themselves into sensitive positions and feed him information. Greene is trying to bring the government down, of course, change the system. Greene and the Progressives will hit me on recent incidents, anomalous occurrences talked about in the fringe press, but largely ignored in more traditional media—these included UFOs."

Natalia interrupted, "I asked, 'What used to be called UFOs, Mr. President? We in Russia always took such reports far more seriously than the Americans, who, for some reason seemed bent on obscuring any details which could have proven enlightening. I should think in six hundred fifty years, if they're still being reported, there might well be something to them.'"

Michael took over, "The President explained that, in another few decades, The United States, in concert with New Germany, may well be able to enter space once again. But, to admit that there is even the possibility of extraterrestrial visitation to Earth would be tantamount to saying that a very much technologically advanced potential adversary could come Earth and do as it pleases. This would put the recovering world population into a panic. I asked him, 'So, there's something to it, then?' He said, 'I didn't say anything of the kind, Mr. Rourke.'"

Natalia interrupted again, "I looked at the Vice-President, who had been watching me. I smiled and asked, 'And, what was it you didn't say, Mr. Richardson?' He said, 'We get things on radar, visuals our pilots spot, stuff like that. With commercial aviation starting to make a comeback, God only knows what people will think they see. This is not a cover up. We don't really have hard data and we don't want to alarm people.'"

Michael took over, "The President says, 'We'll make sure you have access to the data Greene's spies have stolen for him, plus a little more, so you'll be prepared when you get hit with questions concerning the subject.' Then I asked him, 'What are some of the other points you want to discuss?' Natalia told me later she was wondering if Bigfoot would be next... The President spoke again. 'You know as well as I do, Mr. Rourke, that you'll get our party's nomination. You also know that the Progressive Party nominee will be Phillip Greene. He's going to try to draw you out on anything and everything that could help him to discredit our party's handling of the political reins for the last almost eighty years, long before anyone returned to the surface or even thought about it.'"

Rourke had been listening intently, the croissant sat partially eaten on the plate. He stood and walked to the rail of the patio, silent for a moment. Fiddling with his watch pocket he pulled the Zippo; from his right front jean pocket he pulled the cigar case and selected one. Rourke flipped open the lighter and holding the tip of the cigar in the flame, he rolled it back and forth in the flame without puffing. When it was to his satisfaction he brought it to his lips and inhaled deeply. Slowly expelling the smoke, he suddenly turned and faced Michael, "Son," he said between tight lips. "We're being played."

*****

When Michael and Natalia finally left, Emma called Paul and told them they were on the way to see their kids. "Paul, would it be okay if they stayed another night?"

"Sure, if that is okay with them."

When they arrived at the Rubenstein home, Paula met them in the yard and after she physically checked her parents over for injuries and finding none, relaxed. Tim and John Michael played video games while Natalie and Paula locked themselves in Natalie's bedroom to discuss "important girl stuff." John, Annie and Paul went to the kitchen and Rourke caught them up on the happenings of the past few days.

Paul, leaning against the counter top in the kitchen sipped his coffee. "John, what does all of this mean?"

Jerry Ahern, Sharon Ahern & Bob Anderson

"I don't know yet. I simply don't know but it all makes me very uncomfortable. Dodd's reappearance, more accurately the appearance of Dodd's clone was unsettling enough. That he had that tattoo is even more unsettling."

Emma came in with Paula in tow. "John you need to listen to this, tell him Paula."

"I didn't mean to get her in trouble. I had promised not to tell anyone and I broke my promise."

"What promise and to whom?" Rourke asked with concern.

"Amanda, my roommate at school."

"What did she tell you?" Rourke listened with interest, finally interrupting. "Paula, can you call Amanda and have her come over here. I need to talk to her."

"Okay, but she's going to be mad at me..."

Rourke walked over, gave Paula a hug and said, "I'll fix it Baby, I promise. Give her a call please."

Fifteen minutes later Amanda arrived in a Taxi, paid the driver, squared her shoulders and went up to the door to face... what. She didn't know what. Before Amanda could ring the bell, Paula jerked the door open and began to apologize, "Amanda, I'm sorry I didn't mean to mess up, forgive me." That's when Rourke hollered from the kitchen, "Amanda, come in here please. You're not in trouble."

Amanda walked into the kitchen, obviously nervous and not sure if she was in trouble, but thought she might be. Rourke said, "Sit down Honey, you're not in trouble but I do need to ask you some questions." Amanda sat and with a little prompting from Rourke finally spilled out her story about the anomaly. The adults in the room sat silent.

When Amanda finished, Rourke advised her to keep this meeting a secret until he had given her permission to speak about it with others. They called her another cab and Rourke paid for it. When she left Rourke dialed up his son Michael, "Are you and Natalia free right now? Good, I'm calling a family meeting at Paul's; how soon can the two of you get here?"

Thirty minutes later, the Rourke family sat in the living room. Rourke briefed Michael and Natalia on Amanda's anomaly. "Here's what I think

68

happened. The anomaly reveals that, for a period of three terrestrial years, the Eden Project fleet remained stationary, unmoving in space. This is impossible, but the evidence appears to be incontrovertible. I surmise that, while the Eden Project personnel traveled in cryogenic sleep through the void of space, the ships were not only observed, but waylaid and visited by intelligent beings from another solar system, creatures far in advance of humankind. After the brief period of study, examination and experimentation, the Eden Project was sent along on its way."

"You're thinking that was when Dodd was cloned?" Michael asked.

"Had to have been, and probably not just Dodd—it may have involved more of the crew," his father said. "They were cloned without their knowledge or consent and it could have gone on forever undetected if Amada's research hadn't noted the discrepancies and if the Dodd clone had not been killed in the attack on Emma and me."

Paul asked, "So what now? What do we do with this knowledge and information?"

"That my friend is why I called this meeting," Rourke said. "We have some decisions to make."

Chapter Eleven

Had Rourke had the luxury of communicating with one of the aliens, he could have discovered that throughout the history of the galaxies, time had largely gone undefined and unmeasured; time had simply existed. Primitive species only had the capacity to deal with the present. They had no concept that time could be defined in three stages; the present, the past and the future. As a species developed, their sensory capacities increased and "memory" began to occur. Experience, anything in the present tense, could only become relevant with a memory; it was a survival tool enabling a species to remember what had caused pain and avoid it in the future.

Still a primitive mind but a distinct improvement; should a species survive long enough, through evolution the concept of a future, a "tomorrow" could develop. It was a tool for development and planning, depending on the nature of the species, it could lead to growth, knowledge and expansion—or it could lead to death.

One of the first races to develop the concept; learned that having the concept and being able to manage and control the concept was insufficient and almost wiped itself out. They eventually discovered that true strength lied in 'strength of the mind.' This was first demonstrated with a comprehension of the two universal tools for advancement; communication and mathematics. Through these they became the first to also comprehend of and understand a fourth dimension of time—infinity.

As their intellect increased they experienced several levels of evolution. First learning to tap into the resources of their own mental powers, the organ that humans (eons later) would call a brain, began to expand. As that intellect became more dominate and emotions began to subside, their physical bodies became less and less relevant. Sensing replaced hearing, telepathic communication replaced the need for external ears and vocal cords. Mentally controlling the bodies, their life expectancy increased to the point that reproduction was no longer necessary for the continuation of their species; sexual organs atrophied and eventually disappeared.

Unfortunately, they existed as a singularity, no other race they encountered could compare with them. Their insatiable quest for more and more knowledge propelled them through the dark voids of space, constantly seeking stimulation by contact with others. Inevitably, the species they encountered had no more in common with them than single cell organisms. Occasionally, however, they discovered a spark of intellect they could study and investigate. During this period a metaphor for communication and first contact had been developed. The mathematical symbol for pi π with the superimposition of the symbol for infinity ∞ served to open communication.

Pi is a mathematical constant that is the ratio of a circle's circumference to its diameter.

Infinity is a reality that can be conceived only by an advancing intellect. This symbol often opened the door for investigation and study but less advanced cultures often did not wish to be investigated or studied and saw their strange visitors as threats or potential conquerors. Millions of the small physical unimposing visitors were slaughtered by lesser beings when they simply appeared individually on strange planets. Eventually, the visitors realized their numbers had drastically been depleted and their very race was in danger of extinction; yet, their quest for knowledge remained insatiable.

What would equate to 500,000 years ago in Earth time, the survivors gathered together for one last meeting of minds. They agreed they would have to create instruments for their own survival or the quest for knowledge would exterminate them. Mechanical bridges for communications were established, vessels were now necessary because physical appliances were needed for the discovery and investigation of other species and they were no longer physically equipped to defend themselves. Additionally, some species were so primitive and different they could not be probed by mental powers, the data received was garbled and unintelligible.

Once free to explore everywhere and anywhere, they reversed direction and developed what humans would later define as Unidentified Flying Objects. Their symbol was also modified, Infinity, for them had been turned on its edge and a sword was added to always remind travelers of the danger of exploring the intellect of others. They also began referring to themselves by a name; something that had not occurred in millennia. An unintended result of their return to dependency on physical tools and self-identification was the return of specific emotions; the first was self-preservation. Physically impotent, they learned to draft others for their personal defense and eventually their aggression. They were now known, collectively and individually as The Coalition.

Now, in addition to their quest for knowledge they were forced on a quest for resources and now saw certain planets that had such resources as essential for their own survival. Those planets with the most available resources required however, were found to be inhabited. To effectively obtain those resources, often a weaker, less intellectual race was simply exterminated; the planet mined and discarded.

Unfortunately, Rourke would remain in the dark about this information for some time.

Chapter Twelve

The first reports were coming in from the scrolls the archaeological team and the Rourke's had retrieved just before the attack at the wreck site. Several of the amphorae had leaked and their contents had been lost to the sea water but several had remained intact. Many of them, those in recognizable languages were being translated already. Several others were in languages no one recognized and had been scanned into computers that were attempting to decipher their messages.

Most intriguing was that several of the scrolls were not papyrus or animal skin rolls, they were metal. The type of metal had not been discerned but the scrolls were being given a chemical analysis using Gas Chromatography—Mass Spectrometry or GC-MS. GC-MS combines the features of gas-liquid chromatography and mass spectrometry to identify different substances within a test sample.

GC-MS, developed in the later part of the 20th Century before the Night of the War, is routinely used for drug detection, fire investigation, environmental analysis, explosives investigation, and identification of unknown samples. Considered the "gold standard" for forensic substance identification, GC-MS performs what is referred to as a *specific test*. One source identified that "A specific test positively identifies the actual presence of a particular substance in a given sample. A *non-specific* test merely indicates that a substance falls into a category of substances. Although a non-specific test could statistically suggest the identity of the substance, this could lead to false positive identification."

Rourke was sitting in the Mid-Wake Scientific Research Facility laboratory straddling a chair, resting his coffee cup on the chair back waiting for that analysis. He knew that popular speculation has always held that the Library of Alexandria contained the accumulated knowledge of Earth's past, scientific and medical discoveries that were lost forever, perhaps the records of the Lost Continent of Atlantis and other storied ancient civilizations, if they ever even existed. The scrolls discovered in the wine and olive oil jars could detail an intriguing tale of early human history; or nothing of value at all.

That was particularly true of the papyrus scrolls; they could be religious text, scientific theories or shipping records. All had been found before. It was the currently unidentified metal sheets that intrigued him most. First of all, what were they made of; secondly why would someone go to the trouble of engraving metal sheets when papyrus and specially prepared animal skins were available.

He had seen the reports from the first scientific reports. They had classified the Element Classification as a transition metal, density (g/cc): 4.54, melting point (K): 1660 +/- 10°C, boiling point (K): 3287°C and the appearance: a shiny, dark-gray metal. Rourke had a theory, but his theory did not make sense. Of course, he smirked to himself, none of this made any sense. Not yet, he had to wait for the GC-MS.

The machine continued to click and whir then stopped; the enunciator sounded—the printer kicked in. He ripped the first page from the printer, it said the material had an electron configuration of $[Ar] 4s^2 3d^2$. The material was dimorphic with the hexagonal a form slowly changing to the cubic b form around 880°C and it noted the metal would combine with oxygen at red heat temperatures and with chlorine at 550°C. "I knew it, I was right," he exclaimed and rushed out of the lab dialing Michael's number. "I was right. Get everyone together; I'll be there in 20 minutes."

*****

John Rourke had always somehow suspected, mankind had risen and fallen at least once before the Night of the War and possibly several times. He had suspected that eons ago, humanity had reached scientific and technological achievements equal to or far greater than his world had. Now he had something to hang that theory on. By the time he made it home, the others had already gathered. He kissed Emma, Natalia and Annie, shaking hands with Michael and Paul.

"Okay, I have a theory and a piece of very interesting data that could support that theory. I believe that at sometime in humanity's distant past, I'm talking forty, maybe fifty thousand years ago, mankind had attained a level of scientific and technological achievement greater than anything known on Earth before or since."

Michael said, "I have heard theories of prior civilizations that were advanced. History is packed with such theories and our legends have spoken of such things. Dad, what is the interesting data you spoke of that could support this notion?"

Rourke held up his hand with the piece of printer paper. "This report states, and is confirmed by GS-MS analysis, that the unknown metal sheets recovered from amphorae raised from the wreck which sank in the Mediterranean Sea at or near the time Julius Caesar accidently burned the Library of Alexandria back in 48 BC, are in fact made of a material not known by modern man until it was discovered in 1791 by the Reverend William Gregor, an English pastor. And not produced in pure form until Matthew A. Hunter an American metallurgist did so in 1910. Folks those sheets are made of titanium."

"I believe a race of our ancient ancestors stood on the verge of exploring the stars. I don't know if it was because of natural curiosity or the need to explore or a pending set of natural catastrophes they wished to avoid, or maybe they were just bored. I think a fleet of spacecraft was assembled in near-Earth orbit, surrounding a massive space station—which, in the intervening millennia, suffered orbital decay and burned in the atmosphere, pieces of it occasionally turning up in deep dug mines over the course of time, as mysteriously perfect spheres of unknown metal."

"That race had calculated then—as it has also been calculated in the present day—that, by travelling at ninety percent of the speed of light, such a fleet could explore a great deal of the Milky Way Galaxy and return to Earth in one hundred twenty years of ship's time, within the life spans of some of the members of the fleet. Yet, some forty thousand years would pass on Earth."

"The space fleet departed for the stars, whole families among the ships' companies. Humankind's lifespan was considerably greater then, more like that of figures in The Bible. A child of five years old might well live through the entire voyage and return to Earth to live on for several more decades and recount tales of distant stars and the planets surrounding them. Men and women of the ships' companies would age and die, children would be born, become adults, the fleet a microcosm of the great civilization left behind."

Michael stood and started pacing, "Dad, you are making a heck of a jump from the burning of the Library at Alexandria backward in time to forty or fifty thousand years ago back to the twentieth century and then forward to today."

"Look Michael," Rourke injected, "less than seventy years after titanium was produced in its pure form, man jumped into space. Titanium was being used to make replacement joints for men and women. Titanium by itself was directly responsible for more technological developments than any other metal except steel. Who knows how long the ancients had it, what we do know is they had it. What could they have been capable of?"

Michael turned and faced his father, "So what, people have theorized for centuries about lost civilizations, some have been found, most have not. Look at Atlantis for crying out loud, was it in the Mediterranean, was it is the Atlantic Ocean, was it off the Biminis, was it in Antarctica? No one knows, no one will probably ever know. Who cares? Look I told you what the President and Vice-President shared with Natalia and me. I am in the political race of my life, for the presidency for crying out loud."

"I told you, the Progressives are getting ready to examine every shred of my life, our lives. They are going to attack me and Natalia with every lie and half true that bunch of bottom-feeders can uncover or just invent. Now, you my own father have located clones from the Eden Project, tied that to an alien UFO from before the Night of the War. Now, you're talking about what, Atlantis?"

"I don't have time for this, I'm trying to get elected so I can make a difference and maybe, just maybe keep the Progressives from destroying this country like they did the last time. Their abject lies, distortions, half-truths and no-truths at all are what crippled America the last time. Now, they are poised to do it all again. And you're talking about a society that might or might now have lived 50,000 years ago. You are giving my enemies the ammunition that could destroy my bid to be President. I don't have time for this; I don't want any part of it. I would appreciate it very much if you would keep your theories and hunches to yourself, at least until after the election. Natalia, come on. We're leaving." And with that, they did.

Chapter Thirteen

The Presidential Campaign was in full swing. The first televised debate was tomorrow and Michael had been pouring over charts, polls, think-tanks extrapolations and the materials the current President (who was a lame duck and could not run again) and his Vice-President had been funneling to him. He had been briefed on foreign policy, domestic policy, economics, military relations, labor relations, business relations and everything else everybody else believed to be important. He had not spoken with his father since he had pulled Natalia to her feet and walked out of John Rourke's home. Michael felt prepared and pretty confident to meet Phillip Greene and share the podium with him during the moderated debate.

At five P.M. the next day he had arrived at the venue, the Mid-Wake Coliseum and Convention Center. After passing through four layers of security, he and Natalia were in the dressing room getting make-up applied for the television cameras. "I feel like a dork," Michael said. "Make-up is not going to make me any prettier."

Natalia laughed, "You're right my husband, you are already gorgeous." Michael threw a tissue at her. When the time came they were escorted to a waiting position just off stage. They were to enter from stage right, Greene and his wife from stage left and meet in the middle for handshakes from the candidates and greetings between their spouses. This was to be the first time they had actually met, even though there had been constant sparring between them in sound bites and press coverage.

The stage manager gave them the "go" signal and Michael in a dark suit, white shirt and red, white and blue tie escorted Natalia to center stage. She was in a simple, though elegant black suit with a string of pearls accenting her neck. Greene was also in a dark suit, but his tie was power-red; his wife in an overstated outfit that did nothing for her figure. After the greetings, which were cordial, the candidates retired to their podiums and the spouses off stage.

After the moderator made introductions and set the rules for the debate it began and for the first ten minutes or so, actually went rather well. Michael was growing confident.

Then it was Greene's turn to ask Michael a question. "Mr. Rourke, can you explain why the citizens of this great country should elect a known killer to this, our highest elected office?"

Michael stared, "Excuse me?"

"Is it not true that you murdered a man at the age of six? Is it not true that you killed repeatedly as an adolescent and that you, yourself cannot total up the number of lives you have taken?"

"I have never murdered anyone. Have I killed? Yes in defense of my life, my family and my loved ones and in defense of the God-given rights ensured to every man and woman."

Greene pressed, "So, you claim you were on a mission from God, himself. Tell me Mr. Rourke exactly how and how often does God, himself speak to you? Is it not also true you share a belief with certain delusionals, a belief that has never had a single piece of evidence presented in its support?"

Michael was incredulous, "What in God's name are you talking about?"

"Calling on God again for help and guidance, are we Mr. Rourke? In this age of knowledge, wisdom and technology, is it not true that you believe in..." Pausing for impact, Greene looked at the cameras and audience before saying, with a smirk, "UFOs?"

Greene with the bombastic fervor of an old time Southern preacher from before the war, closed in for the kill, "Is it not true that throughout the Rourke's family saga, of which we have all heard so much about, the truth is you were a juvenile delinquent with a killing streak that coveted the woman your father was having an affair with. The woman who shared his supposed journey to reunite with his wife. Yes Ladies and Gentlemen, John Rourke was still married at that time. This woman, a Russian KGB agent, who was responsible in no small part for the destruction of your old world and the restrictions we all now live under. The woman that now shares your own bed, a fulfillment of an adolescent incestuous fantasy. Is that not true, Mr. Rourke?"

At that instant, Michael Rourke realized his bid for the Presidency was over; it was truly a dead issue at this point. Nothing he said would change the outcome of the election. He looked once at Natalia, the color drained from her face, shame written in tear lines down her cheeks. Michael smiled at her and nodded. Michael stepped down of the short dais on which the podium stood.

The dais had been constructed for both candidates so that during a wide camera angle, the two appeared more closely the same height, Greene significantly more "chunky" and shorter than the more athletic Michael. Michael then turned, walked over to the other podium, stood for what seemed a long time looking at Greene and then knocked the Progressive Party's candidate on his ass, complete with a broken nose and several missing teeth. Then he collected his wife and left the venue.

Greene, who in addition to being knocked down had also been knocked out was revived and through blood and broken teeth declined to press charges. He had gotten just what he was after; the election was in his back pocket. He did wish his face hadn't been messed up, but he would "milk" his battle scars all the way to the ballot box.

Two weeks later Phillip Greene would still be getting used to his new upper plate. The dentist had told him that until the hair-line fracture, caused by Michael Rourke's fist had healed, his "permanent replacement dental appliances," namely six fake teeth should not be implanted.

*****

Michael and Natalia were sitting on the patio, a bottle of wine between them but no glasses. Neither had spoken for the better part of an hour. They had finally unplugged the telephone, which had rung insistently since they had arrived home. Michael held her hand, rubbing his thumb back and forth across her palm. He heard a rattle at the gate and rose ready to send some reporter on his way, John Thomas Rourke said softly, "Hello, the house."

Michael smiled and said, "Hello yourself. Come on in Dad."

John opened the latch and stuck a bottle of bourbon in first, "I do come bringing gifts."

"Thank God, all we had was this bottle of cheap wine. I'll get the glasses."

Rourke, followed by Emma and Paula walked through the gate. Emma hovered over Natalia, "Are you alright?"

"Yes, actually I am."

Rourke walked up and kissed her on the forehead, "I'm sorry Natalia. That was inexcusable, not to mention nothing but a pack of damned lies."

"John, you know, I know, Sarah knows and Michael certainly knows better and I pray Paul and Annie do."

"We do," Paul and Annie said as they came through the still open gate. "Hey," Paul said with mock anger. "Who called this family meeting and didn't tell us about it?"

Michael had heard their arrival and had a tray with more glasses. "Hey guys, y'all here for the funeral?"

Rourke spoke up, "Who died?"

Michael said with a crooked smile, "My candidacy, that's who."

"Hope you don't mind Son, thought you might like to have some family around. I can leave if you would be more comfortable."

"You try and I'll shoot you myself, remember I'm a killer. Seriously Dad, I'm glad you guys are here, I mean that."

Paula popped in, "Damn, Uncle Michael, that's a pretty good right you have there. We were watching when you nailed Mr. Greene. It was so cool, blood went everywhere and I swear I saw three teeth go flying. And the look on his face, priceless..."

Michael smiled wanly, "Yeah, but look what I did to my hand." It was still seeping blood from the deep cut resulting from contact with Greene's teeth.

Rourke said, "You know..."

Michael interrupted, "Yes Dad I know the human mouth is a cesspool of germs and a cut like this is dangerous. I've already disinfected it. You taught me well, I'm just sorry I didn't listen better in some areas."

Rourke reached up and cuffed Michael's chin, "Didn't teach you well enough. You should have used an elbow strike; saves wear and tear on the knuckles. Hey, who's hungry?"

Natalia spoke up, "I'm sorry John; we don't have anything prepared. Michael and I were going out for supper after the debate."

Rourke heard a car horn in front of the home, "Paul, can you handle that. Bill's already been paid, just give the kid a tip if you would."

"Done," Rubenstein dug out his billfold and headed back out through the gate.

"Michael you and Emma drag out some plates. Paula and Annie you guys get the drinks started. Pizza in five minutes."

When the others left, Natalia said, "This is nice John, it will mean a lot to Michael. He has been so upset after we left that day. And it means a lot to me."

"It's what family is all about, Natalia. We may disagree among ourselves but it has always been the Rourkes against the rest of the world. Greene better be glad he was dealing with Michael, I would have killed him on national TV."

Natalia smiled, "Michael said the same thing. John, he is conflicted. He feels like he should have done more to Greene. Hurt him more, he's not like you John."

Rourke patted her hand, "Michael did exactly what he should have done, exactly the right way and in exactly the right amount. He did something every good politician, if there is such a thing, has wanted to do since the first debates were televised."

After the two pizzas had been devoured, the girls cleaned up the mess while Paul, Michael and his father started a small fire in the fire ring Michael had set up in the middle of his yard. Rourke had splashed some sour mash in each of the glasses and fired up one of his cigars.

Michael finally spoke, "Okay Dad, I'm sure you have a lot to say."

Rourke shook his head, "Nope, just enjoying a smoke and a drink with my son and best friend."

"No Rourke wisdom or motivation on this the worst night of my life and the end of a promising career in politics?"

"Nope, this isn't the worst night of your life, you've seen worse. Maybe the end of a political career but we'll just have to wait and see about that. This isn't the worst night of your life. Now will you shut up and let me enjoy my drink and cigar?"

"Well, I just figured... You always seem to know what to say and when to say it."

"I do and I did. Shut up, have a drink and a smoke with your friends. Best medicine in the world."

Rubenstein finally spoke, "Well, I have some things to say Michael. First of all, I'm proud of you. You did the right and correct thing and you did it on national television. You stood up to a bully and a scoundrel. You stood up for your wife and for your family and for your honor. There wasn't a man, not a real man, in that audience that wasn't hoping you'd do what you did. We're all proud of you, all of us men."

"I don't remember exactly how John Wayne said it, but here ya go..." Paul stood and switched to his imitation of the Duke, "I'm going to tell you something Michael and I want you to listen tight. It may sound like I'm talking about me but I'm not, I'm talking about you. As a matter of fact I'm talking about all people everywhere. When I came down here to Texas I was looking for something. I didn't know what. It seems like you added up my life and I spent it all either stomping other men or in some cases getting stomped. Had me some money and had me some metals, but none of it seemed a lifetime worth the pain of the mother that bore me."

"It's like I was empty somehow. Well I'm not empty anymore. That's what's important; to feel useful in this old world. To hit a lick against what's wrong or to say a word for what's right even though you get walloped for saying that word. Now I may sound like a Bible beater yelling up a revival at a river crossing camp meeting but that don't change the truth none. There's right and there's wrong. You got to do one or the other. You do the one and you're living. You do the other and you may be walking around, but you're dead as a beaver hat."

John Thomas Rourke applauded and said, "Now Michael, if your political career was not completely destroyed tonight, here's your next speech. 'The folks who are getting free stuff, don't like the folks who are paying for the free stuff, because the folks who are paying for the free stuff can no longer afford to pay for both the free stuff and their own stuff. The folks who are paying for the free stuff want the free stuff to stop, and the folks who are getting the free stuff want even more free stuff on top of the free stuff they are already getting! Now... The people who are forcing the people to pay for the free stuff have told the people who are RECEIVING the free stuff, that the people who are PAYING for the free stuff, are being mean, prejudiced, and racist. So... The people who are GETTING the free stuff have been convinced they need to hate the people who are paying for the free stuff by the people who are forcing some people to pay for their free stuff, and giving them the free stuff in the first place. We have let the free stuff giving go on for so long that there are now more people getting free stuff than paying for the free stuff. Thomas Jefferson said it best: 'The democracy (Republic) will cease to exist when you take away from those who are willing to work and give to those who would not.'"

"Now will you people shut up and let me drink and enjoy this cigar?"

Chapter Fourteen

Michael Rourke had learned that the political climate in America had been controlled for eighty plus years by the dominate and conservative, Representative Party whose foundations were strongly based in the Constitution of the old America, its foundational documents and principals that had formed that country so long ago. Their opponents, the Progressive Party were the latest iteration of third parties that had come and gone since the reconstruction period following the Night of the War. Humankind greatly reduced following the conflagration and continued wars had been significantly impacted, surviving for the most part in either underground or underwater facilities.

It had been a slow process to climb back out of the abyss of near extinction; it had not been easy but it had happened. Now, with the total world population in millions instead of billions life had returned to something similar to pre-war conditions, just at a greatly reduced size.

Man's basic nature, according to John Thomas Rourke, has never changed. He was fond of saying, "You have to remember that the Golden Age of philosophy was ancient Greece. Yes, we have greater technology than ever before, but our technicians have not changed. As part of that non-change, the world still had despots willing to sacrifice everyone else to accomplish their goals of domination and control." The Progressives exemplified that.

*****

Phillip Greene's "advisor" had called for this meeting. They were to discuss the drastic slipping of Greene's polls numbers following the "punch in the puss" as the media was calling it now. The "advisor" spoke confidently, "If you say it enough, repeat the lie, repeat the lie, repeat the lie enough and eventually people believe it. Edwards Bernays and early 20th century progressives perfected the model. There are basically three steps in persuasion; technique in the delivery, spin in the interpretation, and persistence in forcing mindsets. Stay with glittering generalities, bad logic, and bandwagon. If you hold true to these principals, spin takes on a life of its own. Propaganda is an integral part of public information campaigns especially those conducted by governments. The trick is to be better at it than your opponents. You simply have to stay on the positive side between advertising, a form of overt propaganda and what is known as 'covert propaganda.'"

"If, for example, a reader believes that a paid advertisement is in fact a news item, the message that you are trying to communicate will be more easily 'believed' or 'internalized.' Such advertisements are rather obvious examples of 'covert' propaganda because they take on the appearance of objective information rather than the appearance of propaganda."

"To be effective, a propagandist must seek to change the way people understand an issue or situation for the purpose of changing their actions and expectations in ways that are desirable to the interest group. We must control what the people hear and prevent people from being confronted with opposing points of view. We must change people's understanding through deception and confusion rather than persuasion and understanding. Our party leaders may know the information to be one sided or untrue, but we cannot allow this for the rank and file members who help to disseminate the propaganda."

"Propaganda can be the most powerful weapon in war; if it's used to dehumanize and create hatred toward a supposed enemy by fostering a false image in the mind. This should be done by using derogatory terms, avoiding some words while making allegations of your opponent's atrocities. The public must feel your opponent committed an injustice whether he has or not. In other words, lie and lie consistently and tell that lie at every opportunity."

"What most fail to understand about this form of psychological warfare is that it is primarily meant to reinforce the mindsets of people who already believe as you wish them too. If people believe something false, they will constantly be assailed by doubts. Since these doubts are unpleasant, people want their doubts removed and therefore are receptive to the reassurances of those in power."

"If your information comes from an openly identified source, it can be characterized by the gentler methods of persuasion, such as standard public relations techniques and a one-sided presentation of an argument. Identify your information as being from one source, when it is in fact from another. Even better is propaganda without any identifiable source or author. Making your enemies believe falsehoods by using straw arguments. Then attack your opponent, as opposed to attacking their arguments. Be tireless in the repetition of an idea. Develop a simple slogan, repeat enough times; it will be as the truth. Appeal to authority; cite prominent figures that support your position, idea, argument, or course of action. Appeal to fear and seek to build support by instilling anxieties and panic in the general population. Appeal to prejudice, for example, your opponent's father is best friends with a Jew; Rourke himself is married to a former KGB Major. Speak often of your 'inevitable-victory' and that your audience should join in and take the course of action that 'everyone else is taking.'"

"Always remember, to be effective a lie must be the repeated articulation of complex events that justify subsequent action. The descriptions of these events must have elements of truth so a 'big lie' will merge and eventually supplant the public's accurate perception of the underlying events. Present only two options or situations, 'You're either with us; or against us....' And you must present yourself as one of the people; be the common man with uncommon insight and abilities, reflect the common sense of the people. This will win the confidence of the audience by communicating in the common manner and style of the target audience."

"Use ordinary language and mannerisms; clothe your message in face-to-face and audiovisual communications while identifying your point of view with that of the average person. For example, 'Given that the country is going through a dangerous time and the economy has suffered, we should stop paying unemployment benefits to those who do not work, because that is like maxing out all your credit cards during a tight period, when you should be tightening your belt.'"

"Do not be afraid or hesitant to demonize your opponent and his family. Remember, 'They are not like us. They were part of the personality that destroyed the world over 600 years ago. They have killed in cold blood. Their conduct has often been, at the very least immoral. They created the destruction of their own world and now are trying to do it to our own world.'"

"Finally, an attempt to influence public perception by disseminating negative and dubious/false information designed to undermine the credibility of their beliefs. Remember, Adolf Hitler said, 'The most brilliant propagandist technique will yield no success unless one fundamental principle is borne in mind constantly—it must confine itself to a few points and repeat them over and over.' Stay on message. And obfuscate, be intentionally vague and confusing, that the audience may supply its own interpretations. Move the audience by use of undefined phrases, don't analyze their validity or attempt to determine their reasonableness or application. Cause people to draw their own interpretations rather than be presented with an explicit idea."

Phillip Greene stood and extended his hand, "Thank you Captain Dodd for this invaluable advice."

Dodd said simply, "That is all for today, Mr. Greene."

*****

The next morning, Michael was sitting on the patio munching the last piece of pizza from the night before, contemplating what to do with the rest of his life now that his political career had come to such a crashing end. The "funeral party" had not broken up until after midnight. Paul and Annie had left about 11:30. Natalia and Emma were found dozing in recliners in the living room when John and Michael had finished the last of the sour mash. John had given Emma the keys and she drove them back across town to their home on the beach. Michael had covered Natalia with a comforter and taken up Emma's recliner and spent the night there.

His muscles were sore from that sleeping position but when he awoke at 6:00 his head was surprising clear. He brewed a pot of coffee, grabbed the cold pizza and retired outside where he plaintively examined his actions last evening and decided things would just have to turn out how they were going to turn out. He heard the ringing of the house phone and started to get up when he heard Natalia answer it.

Natalia came out, handed her husband the mobile phone and sat down with a steaming cup of coffee, "Michael you have a phone call."

"Who is it; I don't want to talk to anyone."

"You need to take this call," she said sternly.

"This is Michael Rourke. Who's calling?"

The voice said simply, "Please hold for the President..." The President, Arthur Hooks' stage quality baritone voice spoke first, "Michael that was quite a show you put on last night."

"Mr. President, I'm sorry but I could not allow that bastard to slander my wife, my family or me..."

"Hold it Michael. I'm not calling to chew you out. We need to talk and we need to talk face to face with absolute privacy and we need to talk now. Will you meet me, not in my office and not at your home?"

"It will take me a while to get cleaned up; it was a difficult and late evening. Can you give me an hour?"

"That will be fine. I'll have my driver pick you up in his personal car. No one is to know about this meeting, am I being perfectly clear? Oh, and dress casual."

An hour and forty-three minutes later, America's President and a former Presidential candidate walked along the beach on the southwestern side of the island. Michael had greeted the President with a hand shake and the Chief Executive had directed, "Let's take a walk." Neither had spoken for the last ten minutes. "You know this part of the island has always been my favorite," the President said, deeply inhaling the salt tinged breeze.

Michael agreed, "It is lovely..." They stopped near water and sat on some lava outcroppings, remnants of an ancient volcanic eruption. "Look, Mr. President I know my political aspirations are shot. I'm okay with that, I appreciate it but I really don't need a pep talk right now."

"Actually, Mr. Rourke this isn't a pep talk. I want you to listen to me for a few moments. Following your performance last night, I have been in round the clock meetings with a very select group of advisors, they are not sure your political aspirations are in quite the position you think they are."

Michael looked quizzically and started to speak.

"Hold on Michael, let me finish. Here is the situation as we see it. While your attack on Greene was 'unfortunate' and not exactly the way we had planned things; at the same time it appears it may have been fortuitous after all. The polls have gone through the roof, with a significant amount of support for... you. It seems my boy you have positioned yourself, however unintentionally, as a folk hero. Greene, on public television and in the middle of a Presidential debate appears to have committed one hell of a faux paux; he attacked the Rourke family with comments designed to make you lose your cool and do something stupid, which you did. What Greene did not apparently count on was the backlash from his abysmal and blatant lies, and I don't think he anticipated getting knocked on his butt."

"Sir, I'm a little confused," Michael said. "What exactly are you telling me?"

"Michael, what I'm saying is you very well may have won the election last night. It is too early to tell but the media—the ones not controlled by the Progressives—are hailing you as the next Andrew Jackson, Teddy Roosevelt and Ronald Reagan all rolled into one. Greene has made another tactical error; he didn't immediately file charges against you and he has already gone on the record saying he won't— if he filed charges of assault against you now, every-one will see it as a political ploy to take the election. He has cast the die and now is going to have to live with it."

"But Sir," Michael countered, "If I start campaigning again now, I give him a platform to start the attacks all over again."

"This is exactly why you are officially off the campaign trail. Listen, about 12 years ago, the Progressives were just surging to power. Under the guise of 'political correctness' they were able to push through several pieces of legisla-tion. That is when they reformed our welfare program and changed it from a way to help people to a mechanism that created dependency on the government for the 'disenfranchised,' that was their way of 'buying' votes, and it has worked. At that time there were battles going on between the Representative Party, the Democratic Alliance Party and about four minor third parties, one of which was the Progressives."

"The Democratic Alliance started to fall apart after that election, coupled with the loss of the next mid-congressional elections, three years later the Alliance ceased to be a viable political entity—that was when the Progressives took limited power under the banner of 'social change' and 'social justice.' The country has suffered, even with what the Representative Party has been able to do to stem the tide."

"So, if I'm following you," Michael said slowly, "you're saying stay in the race, but don't campaign?"

"Yes, if you drop out now, you'll be branded a quitter—a fighter can't be seen as a quitter. You will have the support of the Representative Party and we wage a campaign of support for you behind the scenes. We can orchestrate town hall meetings, media coverage for the next two months, keeping Michael Rourke's face in front of the people—all under the concept of 'Michael Rourke strikes a blow for honest government' with a shot of you knocking Greene on his butt."

"Has anything like this ever even been tried?" Michael asked.

"Never," the President smiled. "It is totally illogical, however, it is legal and I think we have the support behind the idea to make it work. You just need a plan; that reminds me of an old story about a man that did have a plan, a balding, white haired man from Sherman Oaks, California. He walked into a jewelry store in a local mall on a Friday evening with a beautiful much younger gal at his side. He told the jeweler he was looking for a special ring for his girlfriend. The jeweler looked through his stock and brought out a $5,000 ring. The man said, 'No, I'd like to see something more special.' At that statement, the jeweler went to his special stock and brought another ring over. 'Here's a stunning ring at only $40,000 the jeweler said.'"

"The lady's eyes sparkled and her whole body trembled with excitement. The old man seeing this said, 'We'll take it.' The jeweler asked how payment would be made and the man stated, 'By check. I know you need to make sure my check is good, so I'll write it now and you can call the bank Monday to verify the funds and I'll pick up the ring Monday afternoon.' On Monday morning, the jeweler angrily phoned the old man and said, 'There was only $25 in your account.'"

"I know, said the old man, 'but let me tell you about MY GREAT WEEKEND!'"

"So, I stay in the race but do nothing?"

"Not exactly, you have to nominate your Vice President. Then, the media is going to be all over you for comments; only say something like this, 'I said everything the people of this country need to know about Michael Rourke that night. Do they want someone that will fight lies or a career politician? It is their choice and I've said all I'm going to say, now it is the time for legitimate action and honest government'; we'll help you flesh it out. In the meantime, you stay active and continue your life as normal."

"And you think this could work?"

"I do Michael and so do my advisors," President Hooks said as he clenched his fist and held it in front of Michael's face. "Are you ready to provide a fist full of government, a smaller government dedicated to 'of the people, by the people and for the people' and willing to fight for it? We think it would make a hell of a campaign slogan, what do you think?"

Michael smiled and said, "Sir, don't you mean a non-campaign slogan?"

The President chuckled and stood up, "Yeah, Michael I guess I do. What do you say, are you ready to do nothing and see how this plays out? With your agreement I'll make the phone call and the things we have set up will be put in play."

"Mr. President," Michael stood and offered a hand shake, "I don't have much experience in doing nothing, but I'm a quick learner and I suspect I can do nothing better than the average man. Okay, last point I want my non-running running mate to be Jason Darkwater. I had spoken with Jason before the brouhaha. He's willing and now that he has retired as a Naval Admiral, he is free to run. His record is impeccable and I trust him."

Chapter Fifteen

The morning sun was struggling to break over the tops of the mountain but hadn't yet. Paul Rubenstein watched the view in his bedroom window slowly crawl out of the darkness of night and through the crippled illumination of dawn. Now it held elements of both, he knew in a few moments the darkness would lose and the light would win.

For hours Paul laid awake in the bed not moving; just thinking. No, not thinking—remembering. Remembering the time before; when things were normal. He moved through his earliest memories, through relevant childhood experiences and into his adult life. He went through his careers, his training, his missions and past the point of the airplane crash that had been the start of the end of his peace, the start of his quest, the end of the world and the birth of this new world.

Tears often sprang from his eyes over the losses he had endured and now remembered and for all of the changes he hadn't sought. Once or twice a smile crept to his lips with pleasant memories of friends only to slip away with the knowledge that almost everyone he called friends in that world were dead and dust and had been for years.

Only a few remained, none of them would have survived without John Thomas Rourke. He had saved them and helped carry them through the destruction into an existence none of them had ever dreamed of. The struggles, the deaths were over and a new world had been formed.

Swinging his legs over the edge of the bed he walked to the bathroom. When he finished relieving his bladder he washed his hands and face and stared at his image in the mirror. Never particularly vane about his appearance it was the first time in a long time he had really examined his face.

His physical appearance was that of a man now in his late forties; although he considered himself in his mid-fifties his actual birthday was much further back than that. Now, he sported crow's feet around his eyes, but they were deeper and more pronounced. The crease lines between his brows were now permanent. His hair was a little thinner but not much. Gray strands shot randomly through his hair and eyebrows.

The shoulders were still strong, the waist still slim and he still moved well. He knew he was a little slower but few others recognized it. He was aware his recovery time from injuries took a little longer but it had been years since he had suffered an injury. Since then his time had been spent peacefully and productively.

His days of combat, conflict and conflagration had ended thirteen years ago. Old habits die hard though; he still kept a pistol by the night stand and another next to his easy chair but no longer routinely carried them. His Buck Model 110 Folding Hunter lock-blade always rode in his hip pocket. He still routinely cleaned and maintained his weapons and once a month he continued to go through an active target firing regime. He grinned when he realized how long it had been since the last time he had fired a shot in anger.

Married to the woman of his dreams, now most of his time was divided between his writings, designing civil works programs, teaching and being a dad, "Yes Sir, Mr. Rubenstein," he said aloud. "Your life has turned out pretty well." He grinned, slapped his flat stomach and changed clothes and strode out to face a new day.

The phone rang in the kitchen; putting down his cup of coffee he answered it. "Mr. Rubenstein, how are you?" Randall Walls, Emergency Management Services Director asked.

"Fine how about you?"

Cutting to the chase, Walls said, "All good, no issues or problems. Everything is quiet but there are a couple of ..." Walls hesitated looking for the correct terms. "A couple of interesting things outside our area you might be interested in. Nothing confirmed, like I said everything seems quiet but if you have a few minutes I'd like to show you."

"Give me about ten minutes and I'll stop by," Paul said and hung up. Slinging his jacket over one arm, he adjusted his glasses and put on a ball cap. "Annie, I'm headed over to EMS for a while."

"When will you be back?" she asked without looking up from the computer screen where she was shopping for a new set of running shoes.

"Oh, forty-five minutes, maybe an hour," he said over his shoulder and walked out.

The EMS was only two blocks away and the weather was nice so Paul walked. Randall Walls' office was on the second floor and after passing through security Paul took the stairwell, two steps at a time. He walked past the Secretary, Betty Jones who said, "Morning Mr. Rubenstein."

"Morning Betty, how's Ellen doing?" Jones' daughter Ellen was fourteen and had been injured last month in a traffic accident.

"Better each day Sir, they take the cast off next week and she starts rehab on her leg. Thanks for asking."

Paul stopped with his hand on Walls' office door handle. "Give her my best," he said, rapped once on the door and marched in.

Walls stood and extended his hand and Rubenstein shook. "Come on around the desk, Sir," Walls directed pulling over a roller chair, as he sat back down in front of the computer array.

Randall Walls was smaller and lighter framed than Paul but not by much. Paul always marveled at the way Walls was able to stay neatly coiffed. Not a hair on his head or his neatly trimmed beard was ever out of place. Paul's own hair, on the other hand, seemed to be perpetually wind tossed.

"Here's what I wanted to show you," Walls said as his fingers flew across the keys. Bringing the program up, he directed Paul's attention to the display screen. Leaning forward he studied the image. Finally he said, "Randy, I don't see it. What am I looking for or what am I looking at?"

"These are satellite images for the last three days," Walls explained. "They covered an area about twenty square miles, fourteen miles north east of town."

"Over in the national forest?" Paul asked.

"Just about dead center of it."

"Still don't see anything, show me."

"Look here, here and... over here," Walls pointed.

Paul focused on the screen and slowly frowned. "Are you talking about these distortions?"

"That's it, I can't explain them," Walls said and punching another series of keys brought up more images. "These cover that area from the day before

94

yesterday, yesterday and hourly for the past 24 hours since I first noted the anomalies."

Studying the screen, Paul noticed the anomalies traced vague almost invisible paths across the sky. "How did you even spot this?" he asked.

"Had it not occurred over the forest, I never would have," Walls admitted. "And even then I almost missed it. See how the view of the forest seems to be blocked by something, but not completely?"

Nodding, Paul agreed, "It is almost as if a large puddle of water was moving over the forest. You can still see the trees below, but not as clearly as the trees not under the 'puddle.'"

"Exactly," agreed Walls with emphasis. "I have checked and rechecked my findings and I can't explain this. Here, day one—several of these visual disturbances occurred, always moving in the same direction, from the same direction and ending right here. Day two—the same disturbances, but now from two directions all ending in the same place; day three—more disturbances, multiple directions all ending here," he pointed toward the screen.

"Strange part is I've checked the satellite feeds and ran diagnostics, they're okay," Walls said. "I've checked wind patterns, thermal atmospheric shifts, weather patterns, bird migrations and a half dozen other things. I can't explain it."

Paul frowned, "Can you tell what height these things are above the ground?"

"Varying heights, some appear to be descending, some ascending. Either they appear in the satellite's range at several thousand feet, gradually descend and vanish or they appear at tree level, climb and go out of the satellite's view."

"Any other areas reporting this? What about Space Command?"

Walls shook his head, "Nope, I checked but like I said, had it not been over the forest and if I hadn't just lucked on to it, I would never have seen it or recognized it."

Paul did not recognize the phenomenon, but as he stared at the screens he began to frown. He didn't recognize the phenomenon. He stood up and began pacing, dredging up old memories. He was shifting through his old life, his old skills. Then it hit him, screw the phenomenon he recognized the pattern.

"Crap, Randy," Rubenstein said with a start. "That is an infiltration! Someone or something has or is establishing a base camp right on our front door step."

"Are you sure?" Walls exclaimed.

"If you are sure that there is not some natural condition or phenomenon that will explain what you're showing me," Paul turned and his eyes bored into Walls,' "I don't have any other explanation, do you?"

Not waiting for a response, Paul stood up, grabbed Walls telephone and punched in a code. When the voice on the other end answered, Paul spoke quickly and with authority. "This is Paul Rubenstein. This is an action message. I want the Area Defense Force on immediate alert and ready for armed operations in ten minutes!"

Walls could hear the voice on the other end say, "Roger Sir, prepare to authenticate... Uniform, X-ray, Alpha, Alpha, Zulu, Niner, Six, One, Four."

Paul copied the code down, pulled a card from his wallets and replied, "Authorization code Yankee, Yankee, Baker, Delta, Tango, Four, authenticate!"

The voice responded and in the background Paul could hear a claxon going off. "Roger that Sir, I have authentication and the alarm has sounded. Do you have any specific orders?"

Paul said, "I'll be there in less than ten, have them ready to roll!" Before he received an answer he had hung up the phone and headed for the door. He turned, "Randy, good catch. I'm not sure what you've caught but good catch. Activate the emergency communication system and put EMS Plan X-ray Four into implementation." He headed back to his house to grab his gear.

Nine minutes later, fully armed he arrived at the Defense Force Alert Area. Six minutes after that, he was in the second of six ADF Alert vehicles headed toward...; he didn't have an idea of what they were headed for. In his mind one question kept popping up, *"How do you plan ahead, when you don't know what you're going into?"*

Shaking his head he threw the question out; he'd do what he always had done. Take advantage of what planning he had in place, adapt and overcome, still mobile and flexible. Outside his vehicle window the scene was actually beautiful and peaceful. He remembered another day, so long ago, that of another life, his life, when he was slammed into a maelstrom of events that shattered everything... a day just like this one.

The ADF Team Commander, Captain Derek Reynolds had the heads up display zeroed in on a twelve mile area. It showed the terrain, access roads and for ten minutes he had been issuing orders where his men were to establish their cordon positions. "I want to move the teams into a position close to the center area," he had told his team leaders. "We don't know if there is anything there, but if there is we may—and Gentlemen I say may, have to be able to bring the maximum fire power to bear. We don't know what we're dealing with. I want a soft probe; if we can gain intelligence without engagement that's the plan."

Reynolds, personally thought, *"This is a crap mission. What the hell are we here for? We have no Intel, no mission parameters and, no confirmation there is anything at all here!"* When he turned to face Paul however all he said was, "We're on top of it Sir."

Paul nodded but said nothing.

The troopers were outfitted in the newest standard issue Impulse Protection Systems, dark grey suits with Exo-skeleton appliances. Their helmets boasted heads-up displays that calculated distance to a target, wind and weather conditions, terrain, remaining ammo for their weapons and allowed for direct communication to all team members or selected ones.

Rubenstein wore his standard jeans, leather jacket and his weaponry consisted of his vintage German Schmeisser MP-40 9mm machine pistol with a 32 round magazine in the well. In his shoulder bag he had two 32 mags joined with a "jungle clip" and seven single mags in stitched compartments. He carried the old Browning Hi-power in a shoulder rig with two 13 round mags on the offside. In the small of his back, a Pachmayr gripped 4 inch Colt Lawman .357 magnum; both pistols wore a Metalife finish and were Mag-na-ported.

His Musset bag also held four Safariland speed loaders for the revolver and four extra mags for the Browning all with the "new" Federal hollow points. Instead of a helmet he had a head piece on that was his communication link to the teams and to Reynolds. The six five-man teams had disembarked their vehicles and began moving toward the target area. They moved in a semi-circle that was almost a half-mile wide. By the time they closed on their object they would have closed to a semi-circle of only 100 yards, with two teams set up in flanking positions on the sides.

It took almost two hours before they crossed into what everyone assumed was the contact area. The underbrush and ravines made going slow complicated by the need for silence; the men were focused and ready. Reynolds had deployed "Dragonfly" aerial drones to sweep ahead of the teams. Silent and no bigger than a dragon fly; these had audio-visual capabilities and could provide real time sound and sight to the men at a distance of 1/4 mile line of sight.

Neither they nor the men on the ground saw or heard anything out of the ordinary.

Ground Zero had been defined by the coordinates Randall Walls' studies of the satellite images reasoned was the center of activity. It proved to be an area obstructed by the forest canopy but clear of the underbrush the ADF teams had encountered. The forest canopy restricted the growth of vegetation and had naturally formed a clearing approximately 75 feet by almost 100 feet.

The ADF teams watched and observed from about eighty yards away. Nothing! There was no movement, no tracks, no structures, no vehicles, no personnel they could see and they had a clear line of sight through the clearing to the other side of it.

The drones continued to provide aerial recon zipping in and out of the tree tops; they saw nothing.

After 30 minutes, Reynolds keyed his comm. link to Rubenstein. "Sir, there's nothing here."

Paul replied, "Let's give it a minute Captain."

After another 15 minutes Reynolds keyed his comm. link to Rubenstein and said, "Sir, there's nothing here. I'm going to stand the teams down." Paul nodded.

Out of the corner of his eye, Paul saw something. One of the drones swooped down lower past the tree tops through the tree branches unnoticed. Reynolds spoke into his helmet mike, stood up and waved his teams to congregate on him. That is when the drone smacked into something and scattered to the forest floor; but it hadn't hit anything.

It was flying 20 feet above the ground in a clear space when it hit something that wasn't there. Paul jerked Reynolds to the ground and hollered, "We're under attack, take cover, return fire!"

Six of the men that had already gained their feet were cut down almost instantaneously. Their Exo-suits did not even deflect the attackers' energy weapons. As the ADF returned fire at an unseen invisible enemy the scene of the little clearing was disrupted. Flashes and sparks popped and the picture of the quiet scene shimmered and faded; in its place were vehicles, fixed positions manned by figures in jet-black suits and helmets and carrying a type of weapon Paul had only seen pictures of. Even though the ADF troopers were firing accurate shots, they had no effect on the enemy troops. However, each time one of the bad guys hit an ADF, he died from a blast of energy that ripped a hole through his body.

Stunned by the carnage and its abruptness, Paul leveled his MP-40 on the closest target and squeezed the trigger. He could literally see his rounds bounce off his target's helmet; adjusting his aim he sent a round under the chin of the helmet and above the chest plate his target wore. When the target fell back and was still, Paul thought, "Good, that works!" Just then one of the black garbed antagonists stood up to fire. Paul saw him and fired point-and-shoot, stitching three MP-40 rounds across his target's chest dropping him like a sledge hammered steer.

"Well, well," Paul thought. "Our smart weapons cannot penetrate those suits but good old fashion lead can."

Reynolds keyed his comm. link and ordered the teams to begin their retreat. Those that had cover broke off their contact and started their evacuation from the kill zone. Those without cover were cut down by the scythe of energy blasts.

After fifteen minutes of evade and escape, Paul realized there was no pursuit. Thirty minutes later, the survivors reached the rally point. Reynolds was exhausted from the full-out retreat and out of breathe; his men in no better shape.

"What the hell were those things?" He asked between breaths. "Where did they come from? What the hell kind of weapons were those; they cut through our pulse armor like a hot knife through butter!" After a quick body count, Reynolds realized the ADF had lost almost a third of its troopers; all killed.

Paul said, "We have to get out of here now. We are completely out gunned with an enemy that must have some kind of camouflage we've never seen and weapons we've never heard of."

Reynolds ordered the remaining men to make their way back to the vehicles by the predetermined routes. "Men, however many of you that can, make it back to the vehicles. Your orders are to return to base and sound the alert. That is your prime order! We have to get word back to headquarters—tell them what we have seen and dealt with here. Any man injured or that can no longer keep up is to be left behind. Is that understood?"

Paul stressed, "We have to warn the authorities, or the first fight of this conflict just ended; and so may the hope for our country and possibly the world. That is your imperative and your only imperative, move out."

Paul and Reynolds headed out together. The teams had broken down to one and two men teams, each escaping on their own. A half mile later, Reynolds held up his left hand in a clinched fist. Rubenstein stopped behind him and to his left. They both listened. Reynolds keyed his direct comm. link, "I heard something, but I don't know what it was or where it was."

Paul nodded and moved to his right, further off the trail. In next instant Reynolds disappeared in a fire ball. The concussion from the blast lifted Paul off his feet slamming him head-long into a tree before flipping him head over heels into a forty-foot deep ravine. He hit about half-way down, slid to the bottom and didn't move.

Chapter Sixteen

For a long time he wasn't aware of anything. He simply existed in a universal, swirling all-consuming darkness. Then, at some level of his consciousness, his soul, his brain or maybe his heart; he was vaguely aware of a tiny pin point of light. Each time he tried to focus on it; it eluded him only to reappear elsewhere in another part of his darkness. As his vision began returning, he kept his eye lids shut.

Something said to his returning consciousness, "*anticipate*." His consciousness, responded, "*That's not right*."

Next, he crawled up through a muffled tunnel filled with cotton, climbing higher, and with each step his hearing became clearer, and he listened. He did not know for what he listened; he just knew he must listen. When consciousness came fully to him it came with a wave of pain and agony. He had just cracked open his left eye lid when the wave hit him and he slammed that eye lid shut and willed his face not to show the effort and his lungs to continue breathing at the same slow and shallow rate and with his body not to twitch with the shock.

When that wave passed, he slowly opened the eye lid again and scanned his surroundings. He did not know what he was looking for, but he knew looking could mean survival or death. As he listened, the word "*anticipate*" came again but he knew "*That is not right*."

He slowly pulled his right hand from beneath his hip, flexing the fingers to start the blood flowing. Then he began inching it up the Mount Everest of his body. Cresting the peak of his hip, he moved it down even slower as he crossed his body and up his chest. "*No wet spots of blood, that's good,*" he thought. "*No protruding bones, that's good. Having problems breathing, either broke a rib, cracked it—maybe I just bruised it; think positive.*"

Shifting his weight, he found what he sought. It was hard and cold, but it felt good—really good! This meant life and he knew it even if he couldn't cognite yet on exactly what it was. He just knew it was essential and it was his. "*Anticipate.*" His mind shouted, "*That is just not right!*"

He looked around searching for something important but he didn't know what it was until he saw it. A foot from his hand was six inches of a dark strap; he smiled and pulled it to him. *"My bag!"* he thought with a smile.

Looking around he realized, *"I'm at the bottom of a ravine. I either fell or was pushed. Must have fallen, had I been pushed who ever pushed me would have climbed down to make sure I was dead or finish me off. My bag must have been buried by the avalanche of leaves caused by my fall."* His hand finally recognized where it was resting, "*My Schmeisser, this is my Schmeisser! My Schmeisser and my bag!"* As he struggled to his feet he was staggered by waves of pain and nausea. Finally he stood with feet splayed covered in sweat and shaking with the effort.

"Let's assess the situation," he thought.

The word *"anticipate"* jumped again into his mind. He shook his head and whispered his first words out loud, "That is not right! I'm hurt, that's bad. I'm not apparently hurt badly, so that's good. What do I know? I know this is my Schmeisser and it is loaded. I know this is my bag and it has stuff in it. I know I'm at the bottom of a ravine. What don't I know? I don't know why I'm at the bottom of the ravine. I don't know if it was an accident or not. I don't for sure how I got here. I have no idea of where is."

"What was that other thing I don't know... oh, yeah—what the hell is my name?" Then his head began to spin and his consciousness swarmed. Just as he knees buckled, just before he collapsed in a pile at the bottom of the ravine again—it came to him. *"Not anticipate... plan ahead!"*

Chapter Seventeen

The "blank" lay on the examination table, bright lights illuminating his head. Had he possessed sensory abilities, the lights would have hurt his eyes, but he didn't; yet. That was the next step.

The technician's large and opaque black eyes with no discernible iris or pupil appeared deep and soulful but as detached in this process as the rest of the face which had no noticeable outer ears or noses. There were also only small openings or orifices for ears and nostrils, all of which were located on an unusually large head disproportionate to his body. It was a gray-skinned diminutive humanoid being with reduced forms of, or completely lacking, external human organs such as nose, ears or sexual organs. Its body was elongated, with a small chest and lacking muscular definition and visible skeletal structure. His legs were shorter and jointed differently from what one would expect in a human.

In contrast, the body lying on the exam table was human; in fact an unusually fine specimen of a human male. Strong powerful limbs and musculature coupled with a high forehead indicated strength, power and intelligence but, there was no intelligence in that brain. Not yet, but soon. The body was an exact copy of its original, but without senses or a mind. Early in its development processes those components of what humans called a 'mind' had been downloaded into a matrix then "redesigned." That redesigned matrix was about to be returned to the "blank."

When the final connections were completed the process began; identified by the characteristic spasms resulting when sensory inputs connected to muscle and tissue fibers. After a few moments the spasms subsided and the lungs filled with air for the first time; the transfer complete. The human's eye lids closed and its forehead furrowed, the lights were causing pain, a sign the transfer was now completed. Slowly the eyes opened again and the pupils adjusted. The human stared with a moment of non-comprehension, shook its head and began to sit up with the technician's help and guidance. After several attempts at speech, with no words coming out, the technician offered a sip of a clear liquid which the human sipped, clearing his throat, the human's voice box began to work.

After a few more attempts to speak, the human coughed twice and uttered, "Sir, Captain Dodd, present for duty. I understand my predecessor has been damaged and I must replace him." The technician placed a device on the left side of the former blank's chest mid-way between the collar bone and the nipple. Holding it still, touching the skin, the technician initiated the final step. The device glowed brightly for a few seconds and when the technician removed it there was an image, the device had imparted a design:

Chapter Eighteen

The pictures and video of Michael Rourke knocking Phillip Greene off the dais at the first Presidential Debate had gone viral; the Representative machine had pushed them both. Story after story of how Michael Rourke had "Struck a blow for truth and honesty," were ringing out. Each attempt the Progressives made to redirect Phillip Greene's candidacy ran into a brick wall. "Man on the street" interviews featured in "Michael Rourke for President" advertisements had developed into regular segments on national news outlets. They were even fodder for late night comedy shows on every network.

The Representative election committee continued to flood the more conservative media with the most innovative promotions they could find. Focusing on media outlets that tended to be more geared to the American political right in content, the campaign resembled guerrilla warfare because they knew the Progressives had control of what is said in the national media.

The internet, talk radio and the DOT (Dead on Target) News Channel had led to an explosion of popular conservative news sources. As the conservative media grew, Progressive outlets began to suffer from dwindling advertising, popularity and credibility. Prominent Progressives lamented the demise of a liberal media; and offered support for censorship through legislative means, a rebirth of the threat from centuries in the past, the Fairness Doctrine and financial assistance by means of taxpayer bailouts. It had not worked before and it was not working now.

One recent survey, conducted by the National Federation of Representative Women found that an overwhelming majority of respondents feel the national news media has shown Representative candidates, particularly female candidates, in a negative light. The media was creating the perception that Representative women candidates were inferior to their male opponents.

According to the findings, 89.2 percent of 6,943 responding women (about 5,984 women total) accused the national Progressive media of bias. The rest of the approximately 960 votes were split between those who did not feel the media smeared female Representative candidates, and those who were not sure.

The survey, whose results were sent out to a list of subscribers on August 27th, reportedly asked a total of 8,500 Representative females from all the remaining states, as well as the two remaining American territories, a wide variety of questions meant to summarize the opinions of American women on a broad base of issues.

"Every day we hear the media and others perpetuate stereotypes about Representative candidates, particularly women, about who we are and what we believe," the NFRW website said. "No comprehensive survey of Representative women had been taken to provide data for a substantive response. Thus, the National Federation of Representative Women's Table Talk Survey was born, a survey created by Representative women for Representative men and women."

An NFRW press release stated the data and the overall findings of the survey were, in a large part, economically-charged—indicating that the fiscal policies proposed by the Progressive movement will "fail our entire nation, but women would be disproportionately affected." It stated, "It's clear that we need dynamic and honest leadership right now to turn our country around, back to the direction real Americans want."

Through it all, Michael had remained silent. Request for interviews were politely deflected by the Representative Party's press team. It had taken a few weeks for the news hounds to finally stop parking in front of Michael and Natalia's home in the hopes of a chance sighting of the couple. One lucky reporter had cornered the two one evening as they exited a restaurant; pestering Michael for a comment as they walked back to their vehicle. Michael finally said, "Okay, I will give you one comment." The reporter, a little "Barbie Doll" blond gushed her thanks, turned to the cameraman and said, "Get this and don't screw up."

Turning back to Michael with microphone in hand, "We are here with the Representative Presidential Candidate Michael Rourke and his wife, Natalia. Mr. Rourke, you have been uncharacteristically absent from the campaign trail, are the rumors true that following the..." Michael couldn't tell if she was searching for the right word or pausing for effect. "Following the unpleasant events of the debate, have you withdrawn your candidacy?"

"No Rachael, I have not. However, I see no reason to continue the political theater any longer. Those 'unpleasant events,' and I'm using your phrase, were not unpleasant in the least to me."

"The allegations Mr. Greene asserted that evening were lies and distortions of the highest order. Not only were they untrue, they were insulting. I addressed those insults directly as a man with honor is required to do. While 'politicians' sometimes make their living making 'compromises' a man does not."

"While 'politicians' try to hold on or obtain their offices by slander, deceit and dishonorable actions, a man does not. I believe the citizens of this country have the right to choose what kind of a man they will elect to lead the recovery of our great nation. While I may be involved in a political process... Rachael, I am a man first. I am an honorable man, a truthful man, a man who prefers negotiation when it is possible. But Rachael, some things cannot and should not be negotiated. Honor is one of those things and truth is another."

Holding up his right hand, Michael continued, "This hand will always be opened and extended to people of honor, truthfulness and good will. However this hand..." he closed it forming a tight fist. "This hand also stands ready when the defense of my wife, my family or my country is threatened by someone without honor, without truth; and with good will only when it furthers their own selfish and self-serving ambitions. Have a nice evening, Rachael." With that he and Natalia got into the vehicle and left, it would be the last time for a long time they went out to eat.

Chapter Nineteen

Rourke had received the call from Annie and met her at the hospital. Paul had been found unconscious by a Quick Response Team; only three of the ADF had survived but they had sent out a warning. A two mile area surrounding the event had been cordoned off and a request for re-enforcements from Mid-Wake sent. The re-enforcements were expected within the hour, Rourke knew that time was short.

Paul had regained consciousness and briefed Rourke on what had happened. "John, we never had a chance. Their weapons cut through us like a knife. I saw one of them and they were a match to the weapon you recovered in the Mediterranean. The suits looked similar to what you showed us in the photos. You were right, lead works where the smart weapons didn't but they had some type of camouflage I've never seen. It was like an invisibility cloak or a force field that assumed the colors and textures of the surroundings."

At first, John thought his old friend was delusional from his injuries, and then he remembered just before the Night of the War, he had seen reports of work being done on something like what Paul reported. "Paul, I have heard of research from our old world on something called active or adaptive camouflage. It actually is present in nature. Several groups of animals, including reptiles on land as well as certain cephalopod mollusks and flatfish in the sea have it. They camouflage themselves by something called counter-illumination, but I've never heard of anyone perfecting the idea."

"Well, I'm telling you that someone has," Paul said emphatically.

*****

Rourke met the flight of Marines from Mid-Wake. As the five transports lowered their loading ramps, one heavy assault vehicle disembarked from each along with a contingency of Marines. As they prepared to travel he saw Lieutenant Torquelson and went to greet him. "Hey LT, we meet again."

Torquelson turned and saluted but before he could speak, Rourke pointed and roared, "What the hell is that?"

The Detachment Command, Major Frank Jamison stepped forward and saluted, "General, after the Lieutenant's briefing on the Mediterranean episode we got to thinking. We need some help with this process. Following the initial after-action review of what happened here and the camo issue I convinced the higher-ups to give the idea a chance. General, meet Sergeant Carl Haly, part of a new program the air-boys have been developing called K-9 Working Dog, based on the German Schutzhund program. Sergeant Haly, front and center."

"Sir, Sergeant Haly reporting as ordered." Major Harrison returned the salute and turned to Rourke. "Here you are Sir, what I hope will be our secret weapon."

"Again I ask Major, what the hell is it?"

Haly took over, "This Sir is Gibson. He is a male Belgian Malinois, a breed which originally was developed in Malines, Belgium. The Malinois is prized for his working character and historically the breed has been a favorite of police and the military. They are about twenty-six inches at the shoulder and can weigh between sixty and eighty pounds. The Malinois is extremely fast and versatile. Gibson has acute hearing, exceptional eyesight, and the strength to take down a grown man when attacking at full speed."

"Okay, so Sergeant what does Gibson do, why is he here?"

"Sir, Gibson can hear things no human can, like 'high frequency electronic shield harmonics.' Sir, I'm hoping that Gibson will be our eyes and ears to locate that which is invisible to us."

"Why do you believe he'll be able to do what our people and monitors have not been able to do?"

"Simple, Sir, the human brain is dominated by a large visual cortex; the dog brain is dominated by an olfactory cortex. The olfactory organ in this dog is about forty times bigger than the olfactory bulb in humans, relative to total brain size. He has about 125 to 220 million smell-sensitive receptors. Not only does his hearing exceed ours, but General have you ever smelled ozone around electrical equipment? Well, Gibson can smell it a quarter of a mile away. It has been estimated that dogs, in general, have a smell sense ranging from one hundred thousand to one million times more sensitive than humans. Additionally, I suspect that if in fact the camouflage issue is best on electronic field generation, we will be able to find that frequency by watching the way Gibson responds and know when to search a narrow range of frequencies."

"Okay, makes sense to me. Let's see if it works, I have a hunch we're going to need all of the help we can get. Major, did you get my message about weapons substitution?"

"Yes, Sir, I did. We have retained our smart side arms but all rifles are ammunition based, like the old stuff you like carry. Uh, sorry Sir, I meant no disrespect."

"None taken Major. Continue."

"As I started to say, all of our individual as well as crew served weapons and ammunition are of a... more seasoned persuasion. Likewise, we were able to pull three of the old style mortars out of mothballs and dust them up. Only have a total of fifteen rounds for them. Oh, and we found an old BAR, also with magazines and ammo. Any air cover?"

"I sure hope so, Major. Is you comm. up and running?"

"Yes Sir, it is."

"Then let's make contact with the other elements of this little foray and get this operation in motion."

"Excuse me Sir, but you're not planning on participating in the operation, are you?"

"Major, you don't have enough people to keep me out of it. I suggest we make it to the first rally point and prepare for the ground action. We still have to find something we can't detect and I have been told it is virtually invisible."

Jamison gave a hand signal and shouted, "Saddle up Marines!" and got a resounding "Hoo ah" response. Rourke shook his head thinking, "Some things I guess never change."

It took less than 20 minutes to reach the point of debarkation; it was already late in the afternoon. Major Jamison called over a Sergeant and directed night vision goggles or NVGs should be carried by every other squad member. Rourke wanted to know, "Why not issue them to everyone?"

"Sir, I don't know what we're going into. If everyone is on NVGs and we have explosions or some other dynamic light show, everyone will lose their night vision at the same time. This way I don't have my entire force crippled with a temporary loss of vision that could get us all killed."

"No offense meant Major, just wondering. That is a good idea I probably would not have thought of," Rourke said, knowing the Major had in fact just passed a test.

"No offense taken General," and the Major smiled at Rourke, he also knew he had passed a test.

Three minutes later, the teams had organized into assault formations and were converged on the identified area and the unidentified threat. Rourke was impressed with the silence, stealth and speed which exemplified these as seasoned Marines. Sergeant Haly and Gibson were in the lead formation, the Marines had gone a little over half a mile when Gibson stopped, frozen in time and went on full alert. He slowly put his left foot down on the ground and began turning his head but still facing forward. Haly dropped his rifle, letting it hang around his neck and shoulder on the strap; threw up a closed fist signal and everyone stopped, he re-gripped the weapon and flipped the safety to fire and waited—watching Gibson. He whispered, "Pass auf, Gibson."

The dog was on alert. His hackles were up, and he omitted a low, guttural growl. The Marines in the first ranks had "taken a knee," trying to penetrate the increasing darkness with their eyes and ears. Squad leaders signaled, NVGs and pre-designated troopers flipped them down from their position on the Marine ballistic helmets; the Major was sweeping the area with an infrared detector looking for body images to appear on the screen. Nothing did.

Haly knelt down beside Gibson and whispered, "Do you have something, Boy?" Gibson continued his low growl but didn't whimper or bark. Haly released the clip on Gibson's collar and whispered the command, "Fass!" Gibson looked at his master for confirmation and when he saw Haly's nod he turned back and began to slink silently forward... Then in an instant all hell broke loose and the night sky exploded.

The first energy blasts tore through the night and a Marine's flesh, rolling him ten feet. Recovering, he returned fire shooting with one arm as the other continued to smoke from the impact. He fired a burst into the top of a nearby Acacia koa tree, which resulted in a flash of sparks and a dark suit figure plummeting out of the tree top. Gibson turned in midstride and closed for the attack but the man was already dead.

The Marines were taking heavy fire, the armored personnel carriers were called up and were in position in just moments. This gave cover and a firing platform to some of those Marines that had been caught in the open. Rourke was observing the patterns of fire from the enemy positions. While it was deadly, it was not the volume of fire he expected from a fixed enemy position he feared would be heavily manned. Jamison keyed his comm. link and directed mortar fire on the position. The out-of-date and untested ammo sent three duds in that did not explode on impact but their propellant charges had worked and they tore through the force field and the equipment it protected. That's when Rourke knew he had been correct; the energy field was highly effective against anything traveling at a high rate of speed; like the smart rifles during the fight on the Desperado. Something slower could and did penetrate and would do damage.

His enemies possessed extremely high powered offensive weapons, but their defensive equipment was too sophisticated to protect them. It was like David with a stone being able to defeat the monster, Goliath.

Rourke rolled hard to his left, barely escaping an energy blast and ripped off a three-round burst from his CAR-15, the 54 grain Red-Tip tracers slamming into the belly of his attacker and burrowed through; out the man's back and streaking off still with the tracer compound burning into the surrounding darkness. Grabbing a spare magazine from his belt pouch, Rourke prepared to reload; gun fire blazing from the Marines and energy blasts coming from the no longer camouflaged camp.

The attack choppers rolled in sending walls of 30-millimeter rounds from each of the M230 Chain Guns carried between their main landing gears. With friendly forces in close proximity to the enemy, there was no room for the AGM-114 Hellfire missiles or Hydra 70 rockets to be safely deployed. That knocked out whatever the power source had been, and the Marines could now see their attackers. One of the attackers was sweeping a large energy blast cannon back and forth at the advancing Marines. Rourke saw a blur and realized a team of Marines had penetrated from the left flank and were inside the camp.

The blur was the 80 pound Belgian K-9, Gibson in full attack mode. He hit his target from the right side, dislodging the man from the cannon and knocking him to the ground. Gibson's teeth locked onto the man's right forearm, his victim screaming as the large animal alternately dragged and whipped the man's body back and forth. Moments later the Marines had control and the firing stopped. Now fully encased in darkness the area fell strangely quiet.

The parameter was secured and "mop up" was initiated. In all, twelve Marines had been killed and sixteen more injured. Eight enemy bodies had been found and once Sgt Haly was able to convince Gibson to turn loose of his target; one live prisoner was brought forward. The man's hands had been zip tied behind his back, a painful process with a dislocated elbow a result of the K-9's great jaws. His environmental suit sleeve and right forearm bore tears and punctures from the attack. Gibson was back on lead and stood calmly at Haly's side, his eyes locked on the prisoner ready to take him down again.

Rourke and Major Jamison approached and Rourke removed the man's visor helmet, smiled and said, "Captain Dodd, how nice to see you again."

"How do you know me? We've never met before."

"Oh, I met your 'fathers' a while ago."

Jamison picked a prisoner detail and Haly released Dodd to them. Jamison called his reserve force up, and ordered them to replace the Marines that had been killed or wounded on the line. Medics began treating the wounded and preparing for their evacuation. The enemy dead were stripped of weapons and the camp area locked down and secured. Lieutenant Torquelson, who had sustained a grazing wound from one of the energy blasts, refused evacuation, instead telling a Medic to "put a Band-Aid on it and give me something for pain. It burns."

Rourke set about examining what remained of the camp. After the evacuation of the wounded was underway, Major Jamison joined him. "What do you think about all of this stuff, John?"

Rourke was kneeling holding pieces of a damaged console; he stood and handed one piece to Jamison. "Major, I'm not sure what this stuff even is. I've never seen anything like it before, but I don't think it was offensive in nature. I can't be sure until the experts get a chance to look over it, but I think the majority of it was some type of communications or monitoring equipment. I would suggest that you get this stuff collected and have it transported back to Mid-Wake and let the 'science boys' start trying to figure it all out. What I know is this was the second battle with an unknown force in which we have encountered a Captain Dodd clone; I doubt it will be the last."

Jamison nodded, "I don't think you could actually call this a battle, Dr. Rourke. This will simply go down in history as 'The Fight in the Forest.'"

"Whatever we call it Major, it is not the last time we'll see Dodd," Rourke said with finality.

Chapter Twenty

"As near as we can determine, this stuff was primarily for chemical and mineral analysis," the speaker, Dr. Fred Williams, head of the Mid-Wake Research Institute said as he pointed to an array on the other table. "That appears to be communications and surveillance equipment. None of my staff however is familiar with the technology or have seen anything like this before. Of course, it would have helped Dr. Rourke if you people hadn't shot it all to hell before you gave it to me to figure out what it was."

Rourke smiled and nodded, "Things were a little... intense Doc when we came upon it. Any other information?"

"Not really except, if this is communications equipment, and it is our belief that it is, it is for extremely long range communications. And it definitely did not originate on Earth."

"Any hope of getting any of it to work again?"

Williams shook his head, "The analysis stuff, no way. The communications and surveillance stuff... maybe. It isn't as badly damaged, we think. How long will it take? No clue, we're still trying to understand the technology, but we will continue to try. Dr. Rourke, do you know anything about UFOs?"

Rourke, remembering the trip to Canada before the Night of the War, said, "I know there have always been legends of flying ships and visitors or 'Gods' that could fly. Every culture has those stories."

Williams nodded, "As a scientist I can't discount anything. The UFO craze really got started back on June 25th, 1947. Kenneth Arnold, a pilot, reported seeing several objects while flying near Mt Rainier, Washington. He said they appeared to be in formation and moving 'like a saucer would if you skipped it across the water'; from that report, the term 'Flying Saucers' was coined. Arnold could not identify the flying objects, and thus the age of the Unidentified Flying Objects was born."

"On July 7th, after hearing about Arnold's 'flying saucers,' a ranch foreman named Mac Brazel contacted the Sheriff of Chaves County, New Mexico about some strange material he had found on the Foster Ranch. Brazel was certain it was the remains of a 'flying disc.' Sheriff Wilcox contacted the Roswell Army Air Force base and a base intelligence officer, Major Jessie Marcel, was immediately detailed to look into the matter."

"The Roswell Daily Record released a story on July 8th that said the Army Air Force had 'captured' a flying saucer. The story was quickly picked up by the news-wires and the story went viral. Almost as quickly, the next day in fact, July 9th, the paper ran a story that the AAF backtracked and declared the remains were just parts of a weather balloon experiment that had failed."

"Soon everyone that did believe in UFOs was saying it was a cover-up. One version of the story said the UFO had crashed, another said it had landed. There were even claims that as many as three passengers, alien beings, had been killed; some stories said one was seriously injured but died shortly after and the government had the bodies and were studying them."

"I saw an old report that said in September, 1947, two months after the crash, a renowned astronomer and meteor expert Dr. Lincoln La Paz was recruited by the U.S. Army Counter-Intelligence Corps to determine the speed, direction, and trajectory of the craft prior to its impact. Strange, since the military was maintaining the story to the public that the object was nothing more than a mere slow moving wind-blown weather device. La Paz ran into a 'sea of reluctant witnesses,' apparently hushed up by the government. They had forgotten, however, about the fairly large number of Spanish speaking people in the general Roswell-Corona area. Of special interest to La Paz were those along the suspected flight path, a group that was somehow collectively overlooked by the powers that be."

"Lt Walter G. Haut was the Roswell base public information officer who had written the original press-release. It had begun with 'The many rumors regarding the flying disc became a reality yesterday when the intelligence officer of the 509th Bomb Group of the Eighth Air Force, Roswell Army Air Field, was fortunate enough to gain possession of a disc.' Haut lived in Roswell and became one of the most interviewed and public Roswell witnesses and key advocate of a UFO crash. He always said he thought the original press release was the truth and he was convinced the 'material recovered was some type of craft from outer space.'"

"Haut also left a sealed, notarized affidavit to be opened after his death. In it, Haut claimed the crash site was 40 miles of north of Roswell and that was where the main craft and bodies were found. Haut swore that he had personally seen the crashed craft at Roswell Base Building 84, also known as Hangar P-3. He said it was 12-15ft long, not quite as wide and about 6ft high. It was more of an egg-shape, no windows, portholes or wings—NOT the classic round flying saucer. He also said he had seen short—about four feet tall—alien bodies with disproportionally large heads."

"An Army Sergeant named Frederick Benthal said he was the Army photographer flown in from Washington to photograph the alien bodies in a tent at the crash site, with everybody else cleared out. Two MPs, PFC Ed Sain and Cpl Raymond Van Why, reported they had been at the site. Sain said he had been brought to the site in one of the ambulances and ordered to shoot anybody who tried to enter a particular tent. His son said his father didn't like to talk about it, but had told him he had guarded the bodies in the tent until they were transported to the base."

"Sgt Homer Rowlette, 603rd Air Engineering Squadron, at least according to his son and daughter, told them on his deathbed he had been part of the cleanup detail. He had handled the infamous 'memory foil' and had seen the 'somewhat circular' ship and 'three little people' with large heads and at least one was alive."

Rourke asked, "Why are you telling me this, Doc?"

"Because Dr. Rourke, I don't believe these pieces of equipment originated on Earth, that raises the question, 'if not from here, where?' I can only think of one answer."

Chapter Twenty-One

Dodd's arm had been cleaned and sutured; now wearing an orange jump suit he sat quietly through the interrogation. The interrogation team consisted of Rourke, two military senior investigators and a doctor of psychology, who asked "Why are you here?"

"Why, we are studying you, of course."

Rourke interrupted, "Why did you stage the underwater attack on me?"

"It was not I, it was my predecessor."

"Why did he attack me?"

"My Creator learned about the ongoing recovery of certain ancient documents that might have information my Creator deemed... important. My predecessor was sent to obtain that information."

"Who is your creator?" the psychologist asked.

"Why, he is the Creator."

Rourke asked, "And this information your predecessor tried to kill me for?"

"The Creator was unsure. He believed it contained information about The Others, the time of their return is approaching."

"Who are The Others and where are they returning from?" Rourke asked.

"The Others are... The Others. It is nearing time for them to return from their journey."

"Where are they returning to?" The psychologist quarried.

"Why, here of course. This is their home world." There was a burning sensation high on his chest, Dodd rubbed it, looked quizzical for a moment and slumped over; his head striking the table, dead.

Rourke leaped across the table, laid Dodd on the floor and jerked open the jump suit, checked for a pulse and finding none began compressions. Rourke roared, "Get a crash cart in here, stat." It was useless however, Dodd never regained consciousness, even when the crash cart arrived and the Medics tried three times with the defibrillator. It was obvious; Dodd was dead.

Rourke stepped back to allow the Medics access, he stood back against the far wall of the room pondering what had just happened and the pitifully small amount of information they had extracted from Captain Dodd. As they rolled Dodd's body away to the morgue, Rourke asked one of the investigators to accompany him to Linguistics Section.

Once there, Jose Zima, the senior research analyst, approached. Late thirties, Zima was under six feet in height and stocky. His dark eyes seemed to be charged energy, his complexion was dark and his jet black hair was cut short. Zima shook his head, "Still nothing to report, we have scanned all of the symbols from the titanium sheets and are about to load them into the computer's matrix. It will then sort the symbols and attempt to postulate letters and words but it will be a slow process. It would help if we had a specific word combination we were looking for; the matrix program is fairly intuitive and can make postulations based on common linguistic traits all languages share."

Rourke thought for a moment before saying, "Try 'The Others' capital T and capital O and try 'journey and return' no caps." Zima nodded. Once the loading process was complete, Zima typed the words Rourke had specified, hit enter, leaned back in his chair and said, "Now, we wait."

Rourke, with a crooked smile said, "Mr. Zima, I hope it doesn't take very long. I don't know how much time we have."

Zima smiled, "I don't think it will take very long Dr. Rourke. These computers contain all of Earth's known written languages to include alphabets and pictographs. Languages all follow predictable paths, for example, family structure, agriculture, worship and life are all shared concepts the human mind operates in. Additionally, within the family we also must have 'I,' 'me,' 'mother,' 'father,' 'children' and 'others.' Agriculture contains growth, crops, food, hunger and seasonal cycles. Worship contains God, gods, creation, sacrifice, redemption, etc. Life contains death and birth, you get the idea. To perform functionally each language will have simple or complex predicates and verb serialization, noun incorporation, possessive classifiers, diphthongs, accent patterns, and directional terms. We are simply trying to reconstruct a language none of us know anymore but once was a functional language with the ability to communicate complex information from one person to another. It had its own lexicography"

"For example, the loss of the French quantificational determiners, which agglutinated to nouns, resulted in the occurrence of bare nouns in argument positions. This triggered a shift in noun denotation, from predicative in French to argumental, and accounts for the very different determiner systems of the Creole and its lexifier. The analysis provides evidence for the universality of semantic features like Definiteness and Specificity, and the mapping of their form and function."

"If you say so Mr. Zima, if you say so." Rourke smiled, not having a clue about what Zima just said.

Chapter Twenty-Two

In the two days since the fight in the forest, Rourke had gotten little sleep or rest. Paul Rubenstein was released, a bit battered and bent but not seriously injured. He was still nursing the effects of a concussion, a cracked rib and a host of scrapes and minor lacerations. Annie was in full "nurse mode" and Paul was in slightly better spirits. Michael and Natalia were staying at the Rubenstein home; John, Emma, Timothy and Paula had dropped in. Michael had grilled some steaks for the "patient," who was milking the attention for everything he could get from his guests. Finally, Michael had told him to get his own beer. Paul picked up a little silver bell and rang it. Annie appeared almost immediately with a cold one.

Michael was stunned, "How did you do that?"

Paul grinned and said, "Training my boy. Doesn't Natalia wait on you like that?"

Emma brought John a refill and Michael sat with a look of dejection on his face. "Here I sit with my old man, my injured uncle and everybody has a cold beer but me. And I'm a Presidential candidate."

Timothy Rourke and John Michael, Paul's son, arrived with a beer for Michael. John Michael said, "Aunt Natalia asked us to bring this to you."

Michael took a swig from the bottle, grinned and said, "Finally some respect around here." After the meal, Rourke and Emma said their goodbyes and left. "I am exhausted," Rourke said.

Emma patted his shoulder and said, "You must be. When we get home, let's hit the hot tub and put you to bed."

Rourke asked, "Should you, I mean with the baby?"

Emma smiled, "You are still a fine doctor, Dr. Rourke but you are definitely out of practice in being an expectant father. It will be fine; I just need a few minutes to unwind myself."

*****

Rourke's phone startled him from a fitful sleep, "Yeah, hello... this is Rourke."

"Dr. Rourke, Jose Zima. I think it would be a good idea if you came down to the Linguistics Center."

"Mr. Zima," he said looking at his Rolex on the night stand, "its 4 o'clock in the morning, what's going on?"

"We are getting the results of the transcription from the metal sheet. You were correct, the phrases you supplied were the key to our success; they were a place to start and it worked. Right now, my team is collating the information and we're running cross checks in several areas. I contacted a couple of my colleagues and they are going over the data as we speak. Dr. Rourke, I think you need to get here. I don't want to say anything else over the phone."

"Alright, let me shower, I'll be there within the hour."

"Thank you Dr. Rourke. I'm sure when you see the data you'll agree this is important."

"All I have to say is you better have the coffee on."

"I'll put on a fresh pot and have you a cup when you walk in. Take anything in it?"

"Just hot and black." Rourke broke the connection, staggered to the bathroom and turned the shower on. While the water was warming, he sat on the toilet, peed and rubbed his face. Flushing the toilet he stepped in the shower and speed shaved while he bathed. He put on his street clothes, kissed Emma who was still asleep and left. Forty-eight minutes later he walked into the Linguistics Center and Zima handed him a steaming cup.

"As promised Sir." Zima smiled.

"Thanks Jose, this will help. Bad night for sleeping."

"Follow me, Dr. Rourke." Zima led the way to the private conference room, two other rumpled individuals sat at the table ruffling through two stacks of computer printouts. They apparently did not have the benefit of a full night's sleep either. Zima made the introductions, "Dr. Rourke this is Dr. William A. Sloan, his specialty is Geologic Anthropology. This is Dr. Daniel Gregg, Astrophysics." Sloan was older, probably in his late fifties, early sixties with

122

grey hair that had not seen a comb in ten years. Gregg was mid-forties, fit and well maintained in his appearance.

"Gentlemen," Rourke said shaking hands. "I take it Mr. Zima interrupted your rest also?"

"And rightly so, Dr. Rourke," Gregg said. "And rightly so, this information is incredible. Jose, do you realize what you have found?"

"Zima, has this information been verified?" Sloan asked.

"No, Dr. Sloan, not completely, I suspect it will take another couple of days for the programming to be completed. You're getting this information as fast as the servers make the connections, correlations and extrapolations; it is 'rare' right now, but it is not raw. The other problem is I don't know what sources we have available to verify it. This is new and uncharted 'stuff.' This is a prime example of finding something unlike anything we have ever discovered, and not being real sure what exactly it is."

Somewhat gruffly, Sloan asked, "Can you testify to the authenticity of the metal sheets? This has all the earmarks of a hoax."

Rourke spoke up, "I can. I was there when several of the metal sheets were retrieved from a heretofore undiscovered shipwreck off the northern coast of Africa. The ship appears to be from the time of the burning of the Library at Alexandria. The amphorae have been authenticated as from the same time period. That wreck has lain undisturbed until its discovery; I saw the wreck myself, the artifacts are genuine. No offense, but I don't understand why you two are involved. I thought this was a Linguistics issue, trying to decipher a dead language. Why are a Geological Anthropologist and an Astrophysicist involved?"

Zima said, "I called them in when I saw the direction this investigation was going in. We have been able to decipher much of the information from the first five sheets of titanium but it can only be verified with these gentlemen's help. I know what the sheets say but won't know what they mean or if they are in fact real without the help of these other specialties. John, not only have we started to resurrect a dead language, the stories the sheets tell will potentially re-write human history. This information is giving us a snap shot of a world, this world that we never knew existed. If these two can verify some of the markers, almost everything we think we know about our own history is about to be turned on its ear."

"Jose," Rourke said. "What are these sheets telling you?"

"John, as I told you earlier communication between humans is both an art and a science. Certain constants must be met, that's the science. How those constants are met, well, that's the art part. Human communication begins dealing with the tangible; food, water, life, death, trade and record keeping. Then, if time allows, the intrinsic is tackled; love, hate, religion, etc. What we have on the titanium sheets is not the scribbling of a hunter-gather or a known civilization from the late bronze age or early common era as I would have anticipated from the ages of the amphorae and wreck. These are much, much earlier. Contained on the sheets, in addition to a proto-language we've never seen, are star charts with stars in positions they are not in today and maps that show continental shapes and features different from our world today. There are depictions of animals and flora not seen since the last ice age. This stuff is incredible."

"So, what does it all mean?" Rourke asked.

"Well, I'll tell you one thing," Gregg the astrophysicist said. "A current star chart of today's southern hemisphere constellations will show 25 constellations that appear at different times through the spring, summer, fall and the winter. The southern circumpolar constellations are Carina, Centaurus and of course, the Southern Cross. This star chart we have translated shows positions that used to be accurate but no longer are. This star chart shows us how things looked approximately 40,000 years ago. If this is a hoax, it is one hell of an elaborate one."

"I have to agree," Dr. Sloan said taking off his glasses and rubbing his eyes. "Someone get me another cup of coffee. Jose, if your translations are accurate, this civilization was the prime moving force on the Earth when most of our ancestors were primitive hunter-gathers; before permanent villages even existed. As you know, many species simply vanished during the last great Ice Age, but here we have anatomical correct drawings of several including our proto-type human ancestors and that seems to be a clincher."

"You know that Cro-Magnon man was an early Homo sapiens; the same species to which modern humans belong and that lived about 40,000 years ago. There was an over-lap with another early ancestor, Neanderthal man, who disappeared into the fossil record about 10,000 years after the appearance of other upper Paleolithic populations. This was probably a result of competition with Cro-Magnon or related populations. The youngest Neanderthal finds include the Hyena Den, considered older than 30,000 years ago. Because of these and other finds, Neanderthals have been re-dated to between 33,000 and 32,000 years ago. No definite specimens younger than 30,000 years ago have been found. And here, we have anatomically correct depictions of both species, apparently created by another, more advanced species that met them both."

"Okay, guys," Rourke said his head swimming with new data but no clear picture of what it all meant. "I only got about two hours of sleep, break it all down for me. Where are we at?"

"Here's the bottom line John," Zima took over. "Using your initial search suggestions of 'The Others' capital T and capital O and 'journey and return' with no capital letters; we were able to establish connection with several other lost or dead languages throughout the world and a couple that are still in use. We have discovered several phrasemes or phraseological units or similarities, contextual similarities and so on. We have learned that several of these unknown language's symbols, part of its alphabet if you will, are still in use years later in the primitive Hebrew and Greek languages. Some were even in use in Asia Minor and the Americas. My distant ancestors were Mayan and I found some of the symbols in the few remaining codicils of Mayan legends and history."

"For example, and this may be coincidence but the Hebrew letter 'Bet, Beth, Beh, or Vet' is the second letter of many Semitic alphabets, including Arabic, Aramaic and Phoenician. It is represented as ב. When 'Beth' is turned in this direction, see how close it is to π, the sign for the mathematical standard pi? Anyway, here's the bottom line, with the help of computer programs and the data matrix we constructed, we have been able to decipher much of the information."

"This ancient but advanced culture called itself the KI (pronounced kē). They traveled extensively in their time. They were aware of the other, more primitive humans that were developing and the ongoing geological and climate patterns the planet was experiencing. The majority of the KI culture prepared for an extended journey that would take the main population away and out of danger. Some of the KI determined not to go, from what I can see right now, those individuals literally became the 'stuff legends were made of.' Throughout the remainder of their lifetimes on Earth, they nurtured and guided fledgling humans in areas of social and limited technological development. By virtue of the length of their life span and the comparable shortness of the lives of our primitive ancestors, their influence spanned several generations. I surmise they became the seeds for our human legends of gods, the Titans and most specifically the main lost continents of Atlantis, Mu and Lemuria and the lesser-known ones such as Thule, Hyperborea and Rutas."

"Now here are the kickers," Zima said. "Dr. Gregg, based on what you have seen, where did the KI go?"

"That's simple, based on the evidence it is obvious they went into space. Don't ask me how yet, but they did. Furthermore, and this is a very rough hypothesis—we need a lot more data—but I think it is entirely feasible that we may be on the verge of an historic event. If my gut is accurate, I believe it is probable that as we are speaking... the KI are on their way home; home to Earth."

Sloan spoke up again, "Here is what I think, it is a theory I have personally subscribed to for some time, and I've done quite a bit of research on my own. The resurgence of interest and speculation about the possibility of a once advanced civilization in Antarctica really began again after WWII when scientists started to pay close attention to the issue. That hypothesis seemed to be confirmed by some medieval maps and research of paleogeologists and glaciologists. Russia had been on the case since Lieutenant of Russian Empire Fleet Mikhail Lazarev, in January of 1820, 'discovered' a new continent. Everybody else gives credit to Captain James Cook for discovering Antarctica for the first time, according to our records, in 1773-1774; but could Atlantis have been found or has its existence been acknowledged long before that?"

"Plato says that Atlantis was the size of Libya and Asia together. It is now thought that in those times, Libya meant North Africa, while Asia was the

126

Middle East. If one adds up the sizes of the two regions, one obtains the size of Antarctica without its ice cap. However, according to Plato, Atlantis sank beneath the waves."

"In the beginning of the 20th century, the director of the Istanbul National Museum, Khalil Edkhem, was sorting out a library of the Byzantine emperors in an old palace when he found an ancient map made on gazelle skin. It showed the shores of western and southern Africa, as well as the northern shores of Antarctica. It also showed the shores of what is now known as Queen Mod Land, to the south of the 70th parallel, was free of ice. This ancient cartographer marked a mountain chain there; name of the cartographer was Admiral of the Ottoman Empire fleet, Piri Reis, he had lived in the first half of 16th century."

"Even though the map's authenticity was unquestioned, it was not until 1949, that a combined British and Swedish expedition conducted intensive seismic measurements of the South Pole through the ice cap. According to Colonel Harold Olmayer, Commander of 8th Technical Investigation Squadron, US Armed Force Strategic Command, 'The geographical details of the bottom part of the map—the shore of Antarctica—correspond with the results of the seismic measurements. We cannot correlate this data with the supposed level of geography in 1513.'"

"It was made in the early 16th century, and on the map's margin Piri Reis had acknowledged he was not responsible for the cartography; it was based on earlier sources. Some of these 'earlier sources' could be dated to the 4th century B.C., one of these sources had belonged to Alexander the Great. Lastly, Philippe Boiche, a member of the French Academy of Science published his map of Antarctica in 1737. Boiche's precise picture of Antarctica was, again, of the time when the continent was free of ice and showed topography that our civilization had no idea of until 1958. Additionally the French academician showed in the middle of the South Pole, a body of water dividing it into two sub-continents. This is where Trans-Antarctic Mountains are now marked. According to an investigation associated with the International Geophysical Year (1958), Antarctica was determined to be an archipelago of large islands covered with 1.5 kilometers of ice."

"Medieval maps showed Antarctica with a precision that for 16th century cartographers was very high and even surprising. It has been determined that the data, with a determination of the longitude of a relief within one minute, surpassed the technical possibilities even of the late Middle Ages. That level of precision was not reached by mankind until late in the 18th century, while in some cases, the 20th."

"In late 1959 a historian and professor from New Hampshire, Charles H. Hapgood, discovered a map created by Orontheus Phynius in the Washington Congressional Library. The map, dated 1531, showed Antarctica with mountains and rivers and without glaciers. The Phynius map, made 18 years after the Piri Reis map, showed an ice cap around the South Pole within the limits of the 80th and the 75th parallels; and two hundred years later, the academician Boiche depicted Antarctica with glaciers. The conclusion is obvious: the spreading of glaciers on the southern continent. Admiral Bird's 1949 expedition bore holes into the Ross Sea in three spots, where Orontheus Phynius had marked river-beds. Fine-grained layers of sand were found, obviously brought to the sea with rivers, whose sources were situated in temperate latitudes free of glaciers."

"Let me state that the maps of Reis, Phynius, and Mercator show Antarctica at the times when ancient Egyptian and Shumer civilizations were newborns. Herodotus claimed ancient Egyptians tracked stars more than 10,000 years ago. It is a fact that land nations rarely produced astronomers. The fact that ancient Egyptians were interested in astronomy may indicate that they inherited some knowledge from an unknown civilization of navigators."

"At least one source claimed the Piri Reis map's data belongs to 4000 year B. C., a time, according to most historians, that all existing nations were at a very low level of development."

"My position is that between the 5th and 10th millenniums B. C., there was a civilization on Earth that possessed great knowledge in the field of navigation, cartography, and astronomy, which was no less advanced than that of the 18th century. This civilization preceded our civilization, and it was not an extraterrestrial one. Its age could be several thousand years, while its location was probably on the northern shore of the most southern continent, or archipelago

Antarctica. Later, this civilization may have resettled to the north-east of Africa."

"With the climatic and geological changes Earth has undergone, including large-scale floods, which were regular and caused long-term local deluges, it is probable these disasters have destroyed most of the civilization's cultural objects. Possibly, some fragments could be found in the future under the thickness of ice. It can also be assumed that the survivors of Antarctica kept and handed down knowledge to the ancient Egyptians."

"Therefore, if there will ever be an extensive exploration of Antarctica, mankind will most likely be surprised with the results. If we accept that Atlantis is Antarctica indeed, then we must get rid of most of the descriptions Plato provides. The island obviously didn't sink, it just moved. Or, if you wish, it didn't move during the ice-age, but long before, and while it was still where it is now, it was inhabited by Atlanteans."

Chapter Twenty-Three

Michael Rourke had been expecting the call from his father, "Okay, Dad. Let me hear it."

"Michael," Rourke said. "Can you meet me at Mid-Wake? There are some things I have to show you and some people you have to meet. I don't want to upset you, but this is important."

"Dad, I figured this was coming. I'm already on the plane and we should arrive in about three hours. Meet me at the gate."

"Will do, Son. Thanks."

*****

Six hours later, Michael had seen it all. Dr. Fred Williams of the Mid-Wake Research Institute, Jose Zima, the senior research analyst, Dr. William A. Sloan, the Geologic Anthropologist and the Astrophysicist, Dr. Daniel Gregg, along with select members of their staffs had given a cogent and compelling presentation.

The Medical Examiner, Dr. Ellen Barker described how, the now third, Captain Dodd had died. "We believe his death was triggered by the tattoo. I'm not sure how, but it appears it happened. We're still trying to discover the exact manner of his death. Witnesses said, that he rubbed that area of his chest just an instant before he expired. We have found some tissue degradation but that is all. Captain Dodd should not be dead but he is and I don't know why or how he died."

"So..." Michael began, "we now have confirmed that there is an extra-terrestrial threat; one we don't fully understand. Additionally, you're telling me that archeological evidence proves an advanced civilization, possibly what legend calls Atlantis did in fact exist and they are scheduled to return to Earth. Any idea of exactly when?"

"No," Zima said. "It could be at any time."

Michael stood and began pacing, he mumbled under his breath, "The press is gonna love it." Turning back to the table, "You people are absolutely sure about this... these conclusions?" They all nodded. "Okay, wait here. I have to make a call," Michael left the room. Ten minutes later, he returned. "Alright, here's what is going to happen. Load up all of your data, get whatever support equipment you'll need and whomever else you believe is relevant to this presentation. We're going to Pearl for a meeting with the President, the National Security people and whomever else the President deems necessary. Let's go folks, our transport is revving up as we speak."

*****

The meeting with President Hooks began the next morning in his Ready Room. It had taken about three hours the night before, late the night before, to set up all of the equipment. They were joined by the Vice-President, National Security advisors, and members of the national scientific community and, surprisingly senior members of the Representative election committee.

Michael Rourke began the meeting with the introduction of the Mid-Wake research scientist and his father, who needed no introduction. "Mr. President, Gentlemen, here is the crux of the situation. What we know is this, there has now been a second encounter with an unknown force. In each we have encountered a Captain Dodd clone; I doubt it will be the last."

"Since the Fight in the Forest, these Mid-Wake research personnel have been in an around-the-clock process of evaluating materials from the Fight in the Forest and the initial encounter against my father and stepmother that occurred during the recovery of some interesting artifacts from an ancient shipwreck and determining the relationship between the two events and the authenticity of the artifacts."

For the next three hours there were alternating presentations and question and answers sessions as everyone tried to "get up to speed." John Rourke finally took the podium. "You have heard what we know. Now, let me explain what we think this all means. The cloned humans based on the original Eden Project personnel are being used to carry out reconnaissance, gaining access to and knowledge of Earth's defensive capabilities for selective attacks aimed at destroying infrastructure, both physical and political."

"The immediate goal of the aliens seems to be altering the Earth's atmosphere. Possibly radically increasing methane and thus depleting oxygen to the point where irreparable brain damage is incurred, thus having control of all-but mindless slaves to mine and otherwise rape the planet; leaving the new base the aliens will establish secure against rebellion. They want to reduce the oxygen levels, to between 18% and 6%. Below that percentage, death would result. It appears that those atmospheric changes can be accomplished by increasing microbial populations and releasing already existing methane into the atmosphere through global wildfires. We believe that when the aliens all-but wiped out our proto human ancestors, they didn't care about what they could take from the planet, merely wanted to destroy a potential rival. In the intervening millennia, apparently the aliens have come to realize they need what can be plundered from Earth and all-but mindless humans to provide it."

A phone buzzed at a side desk and was answered by a Naval Commander. He wrote a message and walked up to the President's side, handed him the message and whispered something in the President's ear. President Hooks rose and stood for a moment before advising the crowd, "Ladies and Gentlemen, I'm going to suspend this meeting for a while. Senior military officers report to the War Room immediately. I would ask the rest of you to remain here. I don't know how long this will take, please standby in here and await my return. Dr, Rourke, I would ask that you and your son accompany me."

The President turned and left the Ready Room with John and Michael close behind. The senior officers issued instructions to their subordinates and followed quickly; everyone else sat stunned and uneasy.

Inside the War Room, the President assumed his position as members of his most senior staff filtered in. When the last arrived, the President nodded and the door was sealed. Powerful communication and sensory equipment whirred into life and an Army Brigadier General began speaking. "Sir, our long range sensors began picking up interference approximately fifteen minutes ago. At first we suspected solar interference but we soon discovered that was not the cause. We redirected several of our surveillance satellites and found this..." The General activated a switch and a large screen monitor came to life.

"What is that?" the President asked.

"Sir, we are not sure. At first, we thought rogue asteroids. We were wrong. These objects still too far out of range to identify are apparently traveling together; it appears they are in a formation. Additionally, the entire body of objects has made several course corrections since first discovered, something an inanimate object cannot do. We have no idea where they came from, only where they are headed."

The President said cautiously, "And where exactly would that be General?"

"Here Sir, they are headed to Earth."

*****

It took another several hours before the "blips" were much more than that. Once long range camera range was achieved it still took time before the objects were close enough to make out details. By that time, the President had ordered the equipment to be connected so the Mid-Wake research personnel could view the scene playing out in space thousands of miles above their heads; John Rourke and Michael had gone back upstairs to the Ready Room.

By then it was known that a cluster of thirty-seven independent objects had appeared out of deep space and were traveling together as a unit. Though not physically connected, course deviations were made simultaneously by each of the objects. There was speculation upon speculation about what the objects were, what all this meant and who the occupants were. Was this, the seemingly most comfortable and realistic theory, the start of the invasion from the alien UFOs? Was this, The Others returning to reclaim Earth as theirs? The call and warnings went out to New Germany, the Russians and the Chinese, the military was on full alert but there was little constructive to do; except to wait.

Finally, the cluster of objects had gathered in a geo-synchronous orbit approximately two hundred miles above the surface of Earth, directly above—or directly below depending on your perspective—the continent of Antarctica. As the satellite feeds were received in the War Room they were reviewed by the national security advisors and the military before they were transmitted to the Ready Room where the scientists, John and Michael Rourke were cloistered.

Stopped as they now were, images were coming in from high resolution cameras capable of reading a license plate at the 200 mile distance. Moving the satellites that housed the cameras was taking longer than anyone wanted; the consensus was to stop the satellites at a distance of 150 miles from the object cluster. The General said, "We want to get close enough to see but not close enough to get anybody excited." The two closest satellites were now within range and had been sending pictures for about the last ten minutes, still little more than points of reflected light in the dark void of space. Then an amazing thing happened. The closet satellite, Pegasus 310, shut down its camera and started moving closer to the cluster. The General hollered, "Stop that satellite! Stop moving it!"

"I'm not moving it Sir," answered on the technicians. "It appears to be moving itself." Pegasus finally stopped its movement and the high-resolution camera came back on. There was now a clear image. "Hell, the General said, that looks a lot like the shuttles from the Eden Project."

Up in the Ready Room, the large screen also showed the image. Jose Zima and Dr. William A. Sloan, the Geologic Anthropologist looked at each other. Zima said, "You're not thinking what I think you're thinking are you?"

Sloan said, nodded, "That's what it looks like to me." He and Zima were punching information into their laptops. "Here you go," Zima finished first. "Dr. Rourke could you come here for a minute?"

Rourke walked over trying to keep his eye on the image on the big screen at the same time. "What is it Jose?"

"During the early and mid-twentieth century several unusual gold ornaments thought to be pre-Columbian, from around 500-800 CE were discovered in Colombia, Costa Rica, Peru and Venezuela. It was difficult to determine their exact age since gold is hard to date. When they were first found, it was thought they were zoomorphic—representing animals. However, there was also speculation they were something else; some Archaeologists interpreted them as model airplanes but... Looking at them I was never to come up with one animal that looked like them. Here's a picture of one."

The image on Zima's laptop bore a remarkable resemblance to the image on the big screen. It too was golden in color with delta shaped main wings and a set of small wings necessary for directional powered flight changes in an atmosphere. The body was wide and marked by designs and a tall "tail fin" was mounted on the rear. While not an exact model of the other, they were too obviously similar for coincidence.

"Are they representations of a bird, or an airplane? Is it a plane...well it certainly looks like it to me. It has always reminded me of a shuttle craft, like those from the old Eden Project. When they were discovered there was much debate; were these creations of religious followers who only served their gods without knowing what they are actually doing. Look it has wings, a stabilizing tail, some kind of landing gear, what else do you need? Similar artifacts have been discovered in Egypt in a 3000 year old temple at Abydos a few hundred miles from Cairo, hieroglyphs were found that look remarkably like an aircraft. Now, tear your eyes away from the screen and take a look at this, John."

"John, do you remember me saying I found some of the symbols from the titanium sheets in several other extinct languages including some in the original Mayan? One of those images we call the Feathered-Serpent, or Quetzalcoatl. Quetzalcoatl is always represented as the guardian of treasure. We know there were priests of Quetzalcoatl who took his name; they existed for hundreds, perhaps thousands of years. He is also known as the son of Citinatonali, creator of heaven and earth and mankind; 'The Very Old One' and as the god of the morning star, Venus. The Mayan calendar was developed on the Venus cycle of appearance. We know the Maya adepts were astronomers and the round towers were their observatories. In one of our Codex there are computations involving about 34,000 years, and 405 revolutions of the moon are set down. These writing were supposed to be the joint production of Quetzalcoatl and two very old gods."

"Quetzalcoatl's reign was considered the golden age of the Toltecs. Corn was plentiful and cotton grew in natural colors, not needing to be dyed, this blissful wondrous time could not and did not last. When Quetzalcoatl left it marked the end of the Toltecs and the rise of the warlike Aztecs. During that time there was an increased practice of human sacrifice, which Quetzalcoatl disapproved of, wanting sacrifices to be in the form of fruit or flowers or treasured possessions; not humans."

Punching new instructions into the laptop, Zima continued, "This report printed in THEOSOPHY, Vol. 16, No. 2, December, 1927 shows, 'There was also a famous Toltecan king who bore the biblical appellation of Balam Acan; the first name being preeminently Chaldean. Besides the striking similarity between the language of the Aztecs and Hebrew, many of the figures on the bas-reliefs of Palenque and the idols in terra cotta exhumed in Santa Cruz del Quiche, have head-gear similar to the phylacteries worn by the Pharisees of old and even by the Jews of Poland and Russia today. The seven-terraced pyramid at Papantlan has three stairways leading to the top, the steps of which are decorated with hieroglyphical sculptures and 318 small niches. 318 is the Gnostic number of Christ and the famous number of the servants of Abraham.'"

"Call it Atlantis or Quetzalcoatl; we have just witnessed the return of The Others."

Rourke nodded in agreement, "Now we just have to find out if we can all play in the same sandbox. Wait a minute, what's that?"

Rourke watched the big screen as one of the ships broke formation and moved into a closer Earth orbit and then began a powered descent into the atmosphere. "Well," Zima said, "it looks like we are about to find that out."

Chapter Twenty-Four

Communications between Command Headquarters and the descending aircraft had been difficult to establish; voice communications were purposefully being denied by the descending craft. Written word messages were received by Earth's national capitals simultaneously, these consisted of the United States, New Germany, China, Russia, Lydveldid Island, Australia and the Gallia.

These messages conveyed instructions for world leaders to rendezvous at a set of specific coordinates; those matching the location of the New German capital. The wording was surprisingly clear and concise; while the grammar was somewhat stilted the instructions were clear and delivered in the native tongue of the recipient country.

The meeting was set for twenty-four hours following the craft's entry into Earth's atmosphere. Furthermore, the craft described its intentions to spend the intervening time to survey the surface of Earth and indicated flight paths it would be taking. President Hooks noticed that these really were not true communications. They were cleverly disguised instructions; apparently 'The Others' weren't interested in giving out very much information.

Following entry into the atmosphere it was possible to observe the ship directly for the first time. The first thing noticed was the immense size; the fuselage alone was the length of an aircraft carrier. Yet even with its incredible size, the craft was highly maneuverable. Capable of speeds that enabled it to move quickly over the face of the planet, it also had the ability to "hover" in place; seemingly to just hang in the air. Another interesting aspect was while there were what appeared to be exhaust ports no one had any idea of what the power source was.

The ship traversed the globe in a grid pattern occasionally stopping to hover over selected areas of interest. These include sections of North and South America and several sections of Africa and Europe. It spent several hours suspended above the North Pole and several others at a list of locations in the Pacific and Atlantic Oceans. The strange part was there was nothing below the huge airship except open water at those locations; it seemed the ship was visiting places that no longer existed and were memories only to the ship's occupants.

Then it settled above the continent of Antarctica at an altitude of 5280 feet, exactly one mile. It parked at the geographic coordinates of 90°S, 0°W; the South Pole. Below it laid a featureless, windswept, icy plateau, the ice estimated at 9,000 feet thick. The ship sat there for several hours, unmoving. Finally, apparently in preparations for the world meeting in less than three hours, the ship began a slow rotation turning a full 360 degrees before stopping and moving off in the direction of South America. The journey ended with the gigantic craft hovering just fifteen feet above the airport runway near the capitol building of the New Germany Republic.

Representatives from Earth's governments departed a hanger on the north side of the airport on a passenger bus and drove slowly toward the tarmac. Stopping at a predetermined point, they disembarked and slowly approached the craft. A hatch opened and a stair ramp descended from the left side of the craft and made contact with the pavement. Four beings came down the ramp, stepped off and stood for a long moment, looking around. Finally as a group they walked toward the world leaders. The beings appeared human.

Each was tall, a little over six feet tall; three had no facial hair but strong chiseled features and the short cut stubble on their scalps and posture gave the three a military expression. This race appeared to be diverse. All had slightly oriental characteristics but there was a blending of racial characteristic.

The tallest was almost Nordic in appearance, another faintly Negroid; the darkest appeared to have the Mongol features of some Native American tribes. They were in jump suits of a silvery, metallic appearing cloth; the fourth, older than the others wore a simple robe like attire. His robe was saffron in color, his hair and beard were long and snow white. He spoke first, holding his hand up palm facing the delegates and smiling, "Hello, my children. We have returned." He had a strong clear voice and was speaking English.

Wolfgang Mann, stepped forward, raised his hand and said, "We welcome you Sir, I am Wolfgang Man, President of New Germany may I ask the purpose of your visit?"

The tallest of the others, apparently the second most senior, stepped closer. "Visit? This is not a visit. As The Keeper said we have returned."

Mann spoke, "You must pardon me. It was not until recently we knew of your existence. We have many questions we would like to have you answer. Would you accompany us to a location where we may speak together more... comfortably? If you would like, why not have your crew actually land your craft here."

The second speaker said, "Our analysis shows the weight of our craft exceeds the strength of this material." He pointed at the concrete runway. "President, for now you may address me as Captain." Pointing to the older one, "This is 'The Keeper'; my other two associates will remain here, outside our craft as a sign of trust. Would you also make such a 'sign of trust?'" Mann agreed and designated two subordinate ministers. "Good, then we are happy to join you Mr. President."

Mann had four chairs brought from the bus for those that would remain. The two ministers sat down and gestured for the Captain's associates to do the same but they remained standing, almost in a "parade rest" position.

Rourke came forward, "Gentlemen, my name is John Thomas Rourke. It is a custom among our peoples to greet new friends with a shaking of hands. May I offer my hand to you in friendship?" Rourke had purposefully positioned himself in front of the one called The Keeper. The Keeper raised his hand, a little unsure what to do next. "May I, Sir?" Rourke reached out with his left hand, took The Keeper's right arm and guided it so Rourke could grasp the hand; then he pumped The Keeper's hand slowly at first and then more vigorously, "I am John, Sir and it is a pleasure to meet you."

Smiling, The Keeper said, "John, I am pleased to meet you."

Rourke turned to the Captain, "Captain, I am John and it is a pleasure to meet you." Without hesitation the Captain extended his right hand, his grip was firm and his eyes locked onto Rourke's. There was no pumping this time, just a firm grip as two beings sized each other up. The Captain said, "I believe the term is 'hello'? Hello, John Rourke I am pleased to meet you." After a flurry of handshakes, the Captain and The Keeper joined Rourke, Mann and the delegation aboard the bus for the short ride back to the hanger.

Rourke sat next to The Keeper; he had taken an instant liking to the older sage. Rourke said, "My people are interested in learning your story. There are a lot of questions; we have only just recently learned of you."

The Keeper finally spoke, "Our scientists had been warning for generations that the planet was approaching a series of natural events that would have catastrophic results for our civilization. There were to be great geological upheavals, probable shifts of the magnetic poles and climatic changes that would affect all life on the planet. It had taken many years but we were preparing to abandon this world and take our entire population into space. That was when the enemy appeared, with no warning the attacks began. There was a great war, even more violent and destructive than anything your people have ever perpetrated."

"We had launched several of our ships to rendezvous at our space port, which was in geo-stationary orbit 200 of your miles above the planet. We were making final preparations for the last two waves of evacuation when we fell under a final devastating attack. We were able to launch the majority of our fleet before the final destruction; but not all. There were no attacks once we left the Earth orbit and we continued to watch as long as the monitors allowed. We witnessed the geological upheavals and the beginnings of an ice age, unlike anything in Earth's history, grip the planet. Then we were too far out of range to see anymore."

Rourke interrupted, "Yet, there are no surviving records of the Great War, or of the enemy of your people. I can tell you that mankind was almost totally destroyed and humanity was reduced to just a few survivors using stone tools, clothing themselves in animal skins and seeking shelter in caves. I believe that some few of your people retained the possessed knowledge of your destroyed civilization's wisdom, passing tantalizing bits, snatches of knowledge and tales of great exploits down through the ages as legend, myth and alchemy. Tell me, what was the war about?"

The Keeper said, "What your people call Chlorophyll. The green pigment found in algae and plants, it is an extremely important biomolecule, critical in photosynthesis, which allows plants to absorb energy from light; making it vital for photosynthesis."

Incredulously, Rourke said, "Chlorophyll, is everywhere. Every plant uses it."

"Yes," said The Keeper. "It is abundant here, on this planet but it is a rare, very rare commodity elsewhere. It is essential for the alien race. They have evolved to the point that food, as you and I think of food, is irrelevant to them. However, they still require nutrition. Chlorophyll is an essential part of their diet, it allows for them to break down other compounds that keep them alive. We offered to share Earth's Chlorophyll with them but that was not the course they chose. Co-existing with us was not their plan, they wanted to dominate mankind and reduce humans to virtual slaves who functioned totally at their 'new masters' direction. We did not feel that slavery was an acceptable option."

"Chlorophyll," Rourke said shaking his head. "All of this over something as simple and plentiful as Chlorophyll, that is amazing. I know that Chlorophyll was first isolated by two French scientists in the early 1800s; it absorbs light best in the blue portion of the electromagnetic spectrum. However, it does not absorb the green and near-green colors of the spectrum, hence the green color of Chlorophyll—containing tissues. Its primary function is to absorb light and transfer that light energy by resonance energy transfer. That is how plants produce oxygen gas; it is the source for the O_2 in Earth's atmosphere. Chlorophyll is what enables plants to produce oxygen."

"John, I must also tell you that many of my people consider that Earth was theirs and they wish to reclaim it. They have no wish to destroy humanity, although some elements within the KI are far from benevolent. They consider the Earth to be their inheritance and view modern man as interlopers, little more than what you would call squatters. They remember your ancestors as primitive and there exists certain... biases against all things that are not KI."

"My closest explanation of our society is that it is most similar in structure to what your people would identify as a constitutional monarchy. The last living descendant of the royal line is our leader, but some within the returnees believe it is now time for him to either step down or go away. If, you get my meaning?"

Rourke asked, "Are you familiar with this design?" He slid a picture of Dodd's tattoo across the table, "I found this symbol on a belt buckle I found back in the 20th Century, near the crash site of the possible 'UFO.'"

The Keeper shuddered, "My people know this symbol and we fear it. That...," he said stabbing his finger hard onto the picture, "that is the symbol of our enemy and it is the symbol of yours. I can tell you this, they are both mysterious and menacing; once before—forty thousand of your years ago—they very nearly obliterated humanity. Their goal was to eradicate humanity and seize the planet as a base for further conquest. You must understand they are not human, either in form or emotional makeup. In fact, they are as different from man as man is from insects. They cannot be reasoned with or negotiated with; it is simply a question of if man continues to exist, or will they be destroyed?"

"The KI have kept their identity secret for centuries and some of our elements have been afraid to step forward, lest the aliens, who are our ancient enemy, strike. We returnees are better able to function on Earth's surface than our alien enemies."

"I'm curious, Sir," Rourke said. "Where exactly did you go when you left Earth?"

The Keeper smiled, "To the center of the Galaxy, it is only about 23,000 light-years away in the constellation of Sagittarius. It is an incredibly super dense region only about as big as the sphere enclosing Jupiter's orbit. Sagittarius constellation lies in the southern sky and is one of the largest constellations in the sky occupying an area of 867 square degrees."

Rourke said, "In Greek mythology, Sagittarius is represented as a centaur, a half human, half horse creature with the torso of a man and the body and four legs of a horse."

The Keeper smiled and leaned forward patting Rourke's knee, "We saw many things on our journey but no centaurs."

*****

The cell phone in Phillip Greene's brief case vibrated. Greene knew only one person had that number. Activating the screen that separated him from his driver, Greene answered the phone, "They have returned. Currently their representatives are meeting in New Germany. I am sure your principals want to know that. Please remind them of my help and assistance and tell them I stand ready to be their representative, coordinating their wishes with the humans once their new order has been established." The connection was terminated from the other end, without a response.

Chapter Twenty-Five

The poll results were coming in and the media was forecasting Phillip Greene would be elected by a landslide. Michael and Natalia watched them for about an hour before retiring for bed; it appeared the Progressive Party had won with about one-third of the polling places reporting. Suddenly, flashing lights and a car horn shattered their sleep. Michael glanced at the clock, it was still before midnight.

There was a banging on the front door and a voice calling, "Michael, get up. Get up now." Michael jerked open the door to find his father, step-mother, uncle and sister waiting on him. "What... what's going on?"

John Rourke said, "You don't know, you really don't know?"

Michael, rubbed sleep from his eyes, "Know what? What are you talking about?"

"Son," his father said. "You won, the election is over and you have been elected as the next American President."

*****

The DOT television network election coverage was telling the story. After an initial upsurge, the Progressive Party's momentum had staggered then totally vanished. The last two-thirds of poll results had been massively in favor of Michael and the Representative Party. The Progressives had taken a trouncing, loosing badly. Michael was not even aware the phone had rung until Natalia handed it to him, stepping outside to be able to hear, he recognized the voice of the incumbent President. "Well Michael, congratulations. Remember our last conversation? Well, 'let me tell you about MY GREAT WEEKEND!'"

*****

The initial meeting between humans and the KI had lasted four days, during which time other members of the KI had left their ship from time to time. They had given their specific reports and returned. The general tone was reserved, human scientists and other "experts" presented information concerning areas of the planet that might foster a settlement of the slightly more than 500,000 KI which made up the entire compliment of personnel from the thirty-seven KI ships. The one called Captain had been designated as the primary spokesman for the KI during this first meeting; The Keeper remaining, for the most part silent. Finally the Captain said, "We have learned what we needed to know. Now we will return to our people and discuss this situation with our leaders."

With that the KI delegation rose and were escorted back to their awaiting ship. The Keeper walked over to Rourke, his hand extended. "I have learned John Rourke this gesture is also appropriate when friends part. It has been my honor to meet you and I will look forward to our next meeting." As they shook hands, The Keeper leaned closer and whispered, "Be careful my new friend, be very careful." Before Rourke could respond The Keeper turned and walked up the ramp of the ship. The ramp withdrew into position and silently the ship rose higher and higher into the sky before accelerating to escape velocity. In mere seconds the ship had vanished above the clouds.

Rourke stood quietly, wondering exactly what he was supposed to be careful of. A distant memory came bubbling to the surface of Rourke's mind, an old movie that had starred Henry Fonda called *Fail Safe*. The movie displayed the Cold War tensions existing between the United States and the Soviet Union during the early 1960s. It told how a dramatic series of coincidental events lead up to an accidental thermonuclear first-strike attack by a group of United States "Vindicator" bombers against Moscow, the capital of what was then the Soviet Union.

It was a dramatization of what was known then as MAD, Mutually Assured Destruction. Upon learning that an accidental attack on Moscow had occurred, the President, knowing the severity of the situation, sought a resolution to the matter that would avoid an all-out nuclear holocaust. With this threat in mind, the President had ordered an immediate similar nuclear strike by American forces on New York City. Rourke had lived under the threat of mutually assured destruction, finally seeing it come to pass. He had lived through the holocaust. He had seen threat after threat come and go as mad men plotted the destruction of mankind, very nearly succeeding in their blind ambitions and diabolic schemes. Now, he had a strange sense of foreboding; he remembered a saying from before the Night of the War. "It feels like déjà vu, all over again." He hoped that he wasn't experiencing an event he had experienced in the past.

*****

"The Earth was ours and we wish to reclaim it. We have no desire to destroy humanity," the Captain said. "They may serve us as their forefathers did in the past. The Earth is our inheritance; we were the ones that watched over their bumbling attempts to walk upright, to find a language, to speak. We knew their ancestors as little more than animals snarling and grappling with each other over scraps of food. We were the first great nation on this world. We were the first culture to develop a culture, industrial production. We were the first to develop intellectually, politically and morally. We were the first to transition from savage through barbaric to civilized life. We were the first to develop articulate sounds, music, astronomy, mathematics and science."

"Yes we were the first," agreed The Keeper. "But we were not the only and we were not the last. These humans, like us clawed their way from beasthood into manhood. They are capable, reasoning beings who have earned their place in their own world."

"A world they themselves almost destroyed."

"Yes, they very nearly did but it has not been destroyed. They fought for it; they struggled past their own barbarian natures."

The Captain shouted, "Our association with them must keep our species separated. Familiarity even friendship with them will lead to an eventual blending of the blood lines."

The Keeper said quietly, "Let me read you something; I believe you will find this interesting."

There are certain truths which stand out so openly on the roadsides of life, as it were, that every passer-by may see them. Yet, because of their very obviousness, the general run of people disregard such truths or at least they do not make them the object of any conscious knowledge. People are so blind to some of the simplest facts in every-day life that they are highly surprised when somebody calls attention to what everybody ought to know.'

'Walking about in the garden of Nature, most men have the self-conceit to think that they know everything; yet almost all are blind to one of the outstanding principles that Nature employs in her work. This principle may be called the inner isolation which characterizes each and every living species on this earth.'

'Even a superficial glance is sufficient to show that all the innumerable forms in which the life-urge of Nature manifests itself are subject to a fundamental law—one may call it an iron law of Nature—which compels the various species to keep within the definite limits of their own life-forms when propagating and multiplying their kind. Each animal mates only with one of its own species. The titmouse cohabits only with the titmouse, the finch with the finch, the stork with the stork, the field-mouse with the field-mouse, the house-mouse with the house-mouse, the wolf with the she-wolf, etc.'

'Deviations from this law take place only in exceptional circumstances. This happens especially under the compulsion of captivity, or when some other obstacle makes procreative intercourse impossible between individuals of the same species. But then Nature abhors such intercourse with all her might; and her protest is most clearly demonstrated by the fact that the hybrid is either sterile or the fecundity of its descendants is limited. In most cases hybrids and their progeny are denied the ordinary powers of resistance to disease or the natural means of defense against outer attack.'

'Such a dispensation of Nature is quite logical. Every crossing between two breeds which are not quite equal results in a product which holds an intermediate place between the levels of the two parents. This means that the offspring will indeed be superior to the parent which stands in the biologically lower order of being, but not so high as the higher parent. For this reason it must eventually succumb in any struggle against the higher species. Such mating contradicts the will of Nature towards the selective improvements of life in general. The favorable preliminary to this improvement is not to mate individuals of higher and lower orders of being but rather to allow the complete triumph of the higher order. The stronger must dominate and not mate with the weaker, which would signify the sacrifice of its own higher nature. Only the born

weakling can look upon this principle as cruel, and if he does so it is merely because he is of a feebler nature and narrower mind; for if such a law did not direct the process of evolution then the higher development of organic life would not be conceivable at all.'

'He who would live must fight. He who does not wish to fight in this world, where permanent struggle is the law of life, has not the right to exist. Such a saying may sound hard; but, after all, that is how the matter really stands. Yet far harder is the lot of him who believes that he can overcome Nature and thus in reality insults her. Distress, misery, and disease are her rejoinders.'

"There," the Captain said. "That is exactly my point; the writer was pointing out our course of action. Tell us Keeper, which of our forefathers pinned those brilliant words?"

"It was not one of ours," the Keeper said. "It was one of theirs. These are the words of a man named Adolf Hitler that over six centuries ago plunged this planet into a world war that exterminated people because they did not fit his beliefs as to what was right and good. That is not the way of our people."

Chapter Twenty-Six

Michael's inauguration was just hours away. The security team had made repeated electronic sweeps of the area. Multiple layers of check points had been established throughout the capital. News vans filled an entire parking lot on the north side of the Capital Building. Vehicular traffic had been rerouted except for specific dignitaries that had been arriving since the evening before. A restricted air space had been declared and military aircraft were patrolling the skies. In the waters around the island, an array of different surface ships churned, they were on constant electronic alert of anything out of the ordinary. Below the surface of the waters were submarines. Security was at the highest level in memory.

John and Emma Rourke passed through the final layer of security when Rourke noticed someone he recognized, Sergeant Carl Haly and his dog Gibson. "Sgt Haly," Rourke called out. Haly turned and waved and came over to them. Shaking hands with John and saluting Emma, he asked, "When is the blessed event?" Emma was definitely showing now.

"Not for a while yet," she answered.

"How's Gibson doing today?" Rourke asked.

"He's kinda edgy, probably just all of the festivities I guess but he's just tense."

"Sgt Haly," Rourke said. "Do you mind if I ask you a personal question?"

"Go ahead."

"I don't mean to pry but it seems to me you're a little 'long in the tooth' to still be doing this job. What's your story?"

"Dr. Rourke, I'll tell you the truth. I reported to Pearl Harbor as a salty young buck sergeant, an E-4. I wasn't very squared away. While the duty here sounds prestigious, I thought the duty sucked. After seeing action in the field for over a year repelling sappers and the Russians on a base that got hit eleven times, humping an aircraft with a smart blaster was not a very glamorous duty."

"I had a Master Sergeant, named Carlington. He stood about 6' 3" and was from the South and he still carried and ingrained Southern accent which wasn't hard to tell after he opened his mouth and directed you to do something."

"The Master Sergeant sported spit-shined boots, an immaculate uniform and a perfect flat-top haircut you could have landed a jet on. Master Sergeant Carlington wasn't someone to be trifled with either. He commanded respect and was a strict disciplinarian with his troops. It also turned out that he was a mentor to young enlisted men completing their initial four-year tour in the Air Force. If you proved yourself to the Master Sergeant, acted with integrity and were honest, if you screwed up, the Master Sergeant would back you to the hilt."

"Master Sergeant Carlington played a unique role in my life. The Sarge was a man I grew to admire; not all career or lifer senior enlisted men were of the caliber of Master Sergeant Carlington. Many were venial, vindictive and petty men who used their rank and privilege to make life miserable for lower ranking enlisted men who had no desire to remain in the military past their original enlistment."

"He, on the other hand, was the exception to the rule. As a result of his example, mentoring and tutelage, I was highly recruited by a number of civilian police departments and when I got out of the service I became a civilian cop for a while. I always will remember returning to the base in my civilian police car and rolling up to the kennel only to have Master Sergeant Carlington come out of the office, greet me with a 'Hello Sergeant,' a big smile and a hand shake and tell me how proud he was of my accomplishments."

"A few years later, Master Sergeant Carlington was killed during a training exercise, when I found out about it, I decided my time in the service wasn't over after all and I re-enlisted; been doing this ever since."

"Well, thank you for sharing the story with me," Rourke said and Emma pulled on his sleeve for them to take their places. "You guys stay sharp today. That's my boy that's going to be on that stage up there."

"Got to be a proud moment for you, Sir."

"Like nothing any of us, except him, ever conceived. Best of luck, Sergeant." Rourke and Emma were directed to the VIP seating and seated next to Wolfgang and Sarah.

"Greetings and how are the proud parents doing this fine day?" Rourke asked.

Sarah was beaming, "Just fine, and how are you, proud papa? Emma, you look lovely." John and Wolf shook hands. Wolf said, "This is a most auspicious day for our two families, not to mention our two nations."

*****

Frank Zimmerman, head of the Presidential Security Detail, was nervous. Zimmerman stayed nervous; it was what kept him focused, trying to plan for and anticipate what other people considered "unthinkable." To Zimmerman it was not only thinkable, he knew it was doable. It was his responsibility to put a wall of protection around the President of the United States, POTUS for short. In his late forties, Zimmerman looked haggard. He wore his salt and pepper hair in a flat top because he couldn't keep it combed.

Zimmerman had twenty-seven dedicated agents, their sole purposes— protect the President, prevent any "unplanned events" and, if necessary whisk the President away to safety. His guys were the best, each one a specially trained and hand-picked professional. Expert shots and trained in hand-to-hand, they were in constant movement to detect, access and neutralize any threat or potential threat they might see.

Their jobs complicated by having what amounted to the heads of state from every nation on the planet in one location and all at the same time. Each country had a similar contingency force dedicated to protecting their leader.

Zimmerman, during the final shakedown briefing had told his people, "While there are no suspected problems we are concerned about, remember... There is always the potential for some 'fifth columnist,' terrorist or traitor to act independently if for no other reason than to grab his or her few seconds of fame as the person who was able to kill... so and so. Stay focused, stay alert and for God's sake stay in communication. By this time tomorrow people, we will have a new President; between now and then be observant, be professional and be ready."

According to Section 1, Article II of the US Constitution, before the "President can enter on the execution of his office, he shall take the following oath or affirmation: 'I do solemnly swear (or affirm) that I will faithfully execute the office of President of the United States, and will to the best of my ability, preserve, protect, and defend the Constitution of the United States.'"

Beginning with the first inauguration of George Washington in 1789, the oath has almost always been administered by a Justice from the Supreme Court. The most notable exception being Calvin Coolidge in 1923, he was administered the oath by his father John, a Notary Public at his father's home in Vermont. Michael Rourke had opted for the traditional method. Standing tall and handsome with Natalia by his side, Michael recited the words read by the Chief Justice and became the next in a long timeline to be called "Mr. President."

Zimmerman's ear piece crackled as Michael and the Chief Justice shook hands. He kissed Natalia, smiled at his family and stepped to the microphone. Zimmerman frowned and started moving toward Michael. He gave the signal and three of his people enveloped Michael, one of the saying, "We have to go Mr. President, NOW!"

At that moment, there was a loud explosion outside on the opposite side of the venue and small arms fire erupted outside. Immediately, a cacophony of returning fire resulted. John Thomas and Wolf Mann were standing now, following the New German security detachment, breaking through the crowd and pulling their wives behind them. The Presidential Security Teams were operating on a pre-planned evacuation scenario. Regular security personnel were directing other people to the exits.

The energy blast ripped the entire domed roof from the building, exploding it into fragments that rained down on the people inside; two hundred alone dying in that instant. Apparently, several individuals within the crowd inside were now firing energy weapons into this crowd; the death toll was going to be staggering.

Overhead, above the city, American fighter jets were dog fighting several unusual air craft. The strange silver craft were each approximately 15ft long, not quite as wide and about 6ft high, were slightly egg-shaped and had no windows, portholes or wings. Energy beams and blasts pulsed from a variety of locations around the crafts' rims. The American fighter planes' smart weapons had proven totally ineffective and they had switched to their retro-fitted armament of missiles and cannon fire.

On the ground, still inside the capital building, Zimmerman's team and that of Wolfgang Mann secured a safe area on the basement floor and were regrouping. Their exit plan had been blocked when part of the exploding roof had crashed through the ground floor, continued slamming into the underground parking garage and crushed three armored SUVs. Zimmerman approached his new President, "Sorry about this Sir, hell of a first day on the job, isn't it?"

"You could say that, Frank. What's the plan?"

"We have to get you out of here, Sir."

"Apparently a heavily armed air and ground assault team is attempting to murder the assembled world leaders, you included. There is an air battle going on above us and an undetermined number of enemy agents are in the Capital Building now, engaging our people. It appears they had prepositioned a secret cache of weapons that went undiscovered during our sweeps of the building; probably had some type of electronic dampeners around them. Don't know how yet, but that appears to be the situation. There are incoming reports that the Russian Premier has been killed along with several in his delegation. We have no contact with the Chinese delegation at all. The rest of the VIPs are cut off in the east wing and the thousands of ordinary people, both in and surrounding the auditorium are caught in the crossfire. It is going to be a bloodbath."

"Dad ... Dad where are you?" Michael shouted for Rourke.

Pushing his way through people, John appeared at Michael's side. "How bad is it?"

Michael turned and waved Wolf over, Michael nodded to Zimmerman and said, "Give them a quick situation report, don't leave anything out. Have we any more weapons down here?"

Zimmerman began briefing John and Mann, fished a set of keys from his pocket and handed them to his second-in-command. "Open the armory." The man moved to the wall, hit a switch opening a hidden panel. Seven of the smart rifles and 13 of the remodeled M-16 A-12s were produced. Michael grabbed for one of the M-16s, the security man said, "Sir, you can't do that, that is our job."

Michael cleared the weapon, inserted a full magazine and jacked a round into the chamber before thumbing the safety on. "Right now, we're all in the fight. Frank, here's what we're going to do. I want five men from your team and five from my step-father's to stay here and protect my wife, mother and step-mother. The rest of us are going to punch a hole through this mess and find a new way outta here."

Wolf Mann and John Rourke nodded their approvals. John and Wolf were now armed with A-12's; two of Wolf's people had provided side arms. Rourke picked a stainless .45 and pocketed three magazines, "Not a Detonics, but right now beggars can't be picky."

The three men went to where their wives stood. "Okay, ladies, here's the deal and we don't have time to argue," John told them. "We are leaving ten men, five from Michael's security team and five from Wolf's; you are to stay here under their protection."

Michael held up his hand when Natalia started to protest. "Hold it, this is not a negotiation. Emma is pregnant, and we don't have enough weapons to go around. We have little information on the enemy forces and no way to evacuate us out of here. You're staying here, it is final. We're going to fight a way out of here or none of us are going to make it."

John kissed Emma, "Michael said it pretty well, you're primary job right now is to take care of the baby. I'll be back as soon as I can."

Sarah, reached for Emma's hand and said, "We'll be waiting right here." For a minute Rourke just looked into her eyes, then Sarah smiled and said, "Be careful."

Wolf kissed the three women and introduced his head of security to Natalia and Emma, "This is Hans Lugar. Do what he says, exactly what he says." Wolf turned and joined Rourke and Michael. "Let's do this, Gentlemen."

Zimmerman led the way out into the hall toward the stairwell that headed up from the basement. Rourke waited until he heard the lock engage in the door behind which ten men were guarding three women, ready to die if necessary in that mission; then he hurried to the front of the men moving down the hallway.

The two teams had separated, one along each wall; people that had trained together fought better together. Rourke remarked in his own head, *"Michael is in charge now, not you. You do your job and let him do his."* John smiled at the thought and more than anything else, nodded, again to himself.

The hallway leading to the stairwell fifty feet away was clear except for smoke settling from the upper floor. Zimmerman was on the left and John Rourke now was leading the group on the right side of the hallway. As they approached within ten feet of the stairwell, they halted.

Zimmerman edged closer to the opening and John moved to that side following behind the Team Leader. The first energy blast flashed down the stairwell, hit the floor exploding, and showered the men with debris. Zimmerman returned fire, simply sticking his weapon around the corner aiming high and squeezing off a burst. He was rewarded when a bullet-riddled body tumbled down; landing in the hole the energy weapon had gouged in the floor.

Of the ten rounds or so Zimmerman had cut loose, Rourke counted five hits in the chest and it looked that two or three more had destroyed the man's face. Rourke looked at Zimmerman and said, "You're either real good or awfully lucky."

Zimmerman flashed a smile, "I'd rather be lucky than good any day." Rourke and one of Wolf's men got set and charged the stairwell taking the steps two at a time before landing flat on their stomachs; eight feet short of the landing, beginning to inch slowly to the top. Rourke was now on the left side of the stairwell and Wolf's man was on the right; both totally exposed but ready. Clearing the way ahead they focused on each other's side being able to see further in those directions than they could on their own side.

Surprisingly the way seemed clear. Taking up security positions Rourke waved and the main body moved up quickly out of the stairwell and on to the ground floor of the Capital Building. They congregated in front of a partial wall and counter being used as an information center. The smoke was much more prevalent on this floor. The teams established security to all sides. Zimmerman activated his radio and got a report. "The Chinese delegation has been located, they are safe. We have confirmation that the Russian Premier, his wife and three of his party did not make it. We have a squad of Marines approaching our positions from the west and we are to wait here and link up with them."

Michael asked, "How bad are the casualties?"

"Unknown counts right now, it will probably take days before we know the finals. We lost three planes; civilian casualties are going to be high."

As he edged around the corner of the wall for a look, an energy blast ripped the rifle from John Rourke's hand sending it in one direction and Rourke in another; stunned. The security team scrambled but had not seen where the shot had come from; they had a sniper. Rourke lay in the middle of the floor, totally exposed.

The sniper was using Rourke as bait Wolfgang Mann thought as he studied Rourke. "He's still alive, he's breathing. From the angle of the shot I believe the gunman is above us and to the left." Zimmerman repositioned two of his people. Wolf stood and quickly popped his head past the cover and barely missed getting his head removed by the shot. "Yes, above and to the left."

Three shots rang out from behind them; Zimmerman spun to return fire. It was Rourke; sitting on his rear with his arm at full extension and a smoking .45 in his right hand. "Thanks Wolf. That was exactly the kind of distraction I needed." The security people spun toward the noise of boots running toward them. Zimmerman lowered his weapon and smiled, "Finally," he said. "The Marines have landed."

*****

The media slowly crawled out of their stunned submissive state immediately following the attack and began to set up their cameras. The Marine detachment had gone down into the basement, retrieving Sarah, Emma and Natalia and their ten guards. When they had joined Michael and the others, the entire group moved to the section of the building the Marines had breached upon entry. Before Michael was ready to exit, Zimmerman sent out three combined security teams to sweep the outside for any remaining threats.

Michael insisted the women and others should be escorted out first, he went to a rest room and cleaned some, but not all of the grime off his face and hands. He thought about combing his hair but decided just to run his fingers through it. His jacket breast pocket was torn but amazingly his white shirt was still pristine.

Then he walked, alone out of the capital, still carrying the M-16 A12. Smoke was still evident on the horizon from the downed fighters. He turned and surveyed the damage to the Capital Building, one wing still stood apparently undamaged, the dome and other wing were in ruins. He turned and saw the cameras for the first time; then he saw HIM. Phillip Greene.

Greene had cornered a news crew and was talking non-stop. As Michael approached he could hear Greene's rant. "Do you see what you have done with this farce of an election? Barely inaugurated and we have the Rourke gang back in action and the capital building in ruins. This is what you fools have brought us. The Progressives promised peace and prosperity, now you have this."

Greene became aware of Michael walking toward him and ratcheted up the rhetoric, "See, here he comes, now. President Gun Fighter, how many did you manage to take out today, Mr. President? How many innocent lives ended today because of you? Look at you, still carrying a loaded weapon. How many did you kill today Sir?"

Michael looked at the rifle for the first time. He actually had forgotten he had it with him. He saw his father standing there. John stepped forward and Michael held out the weapon for John to take and turned to face Greene. As soon as he felt the rifle leave his grasp, Michael completed his first "official" act as President of the United States.

He pivoted slightly and driving with a well-executed elbow strike knocked Phillip Greene flat on his ass for the second time. This time breaking Greene's jaw in one place and dislocating it in another.

Michael turned to the camera, "Ladies and Gentlemen, my fellow Americans. Today, our land was attacked in a vicious and unexpected manner by cowards yet to be fully identified. Our friends have been attacked, our families have been attacked; I fear our world may have been attacked. It is too early to fully assess our situation or our options. I can tell you this; this attack will not go unpunished. I can tell you this also, it is time for us to come together."

"Not just as Americans but as citizens of one world, for the first time. I believe we are now facing a threat that in and of itself is greater than any we have known. In mankind's history we have stood as men against men, nations against nations, religions against religions. We have stood as both slaves and slave owners and we very nearly destroyed ourselves."

"Now, we must stand together as free human beings, for the first time— because if we don't, we may never have that opportunity again. History is written, we cannot change it. We can however, change what we learned from that history."

"Yesterday, we stood apart. Today, we learned we cannot do that any longer. Tomorrow, let nation stand with nation; citizen stand with citizen, brother stand with brother and let us not be shy any longer."

Epilogue

The first reports were coming in. Of the eight American fighters that scrambled, two had been lost along with their two-man crews in air-to-air combat. Two more had been severely damaged and unable to return to base, their crews had safely ejected. The resulting crashes were responsible for over sixty deaths on the ground, either from falling debris, shrapnel from explosions or fire. The fires caused had devastated a large section of the downtown area and a suburban neighborhood on the outskirts of town. The major fires were still burning but were expected to be under control within the next two hours. Flaming debris was scattered from one end of the Capital to the other.

The remaining four fighter jets eventually returned to their base; they remained on station flying Combat Air Patrols over Honolulu until relieved by another flight. Three news choppers became entangled with the aerial battle. One was destroyed in midflight by an energy blast, a second received damage when it flew in the explosive debris of the first fighter shot down, when it disintegrated in flight, the third landed almost immediately in an intersection downtown and escaped being shot down. That pilot, realizing the danger he was in dropped his chopper almost straight down in a dive—he was barely able to stop. It was a "hard landing" that crumpled the landing skids and broke his back.

One airliner that had taken off just seconds before the start of the aerial dog fight tried evasive maneuvers without sufficient speed or altitude and crashed; killing all 228 onboard and spraying hundreds of gallons of flaming jet fuel across one subdivision. Twenty-seven homes and one school had been incinerated. Within the homes, seventeen parents and twenty-one children below school age perished. In the school 1,018 students and teachers suffocated when the fire sucked the oxygen out of the school. The only survivors were the football team and band members who were at a neighboring school preparing for a championship game.

Of the four attacking enemy aircraft, three were shot down and one was missing. Crash sites were declared National Security Areas and investigators were pouring over those locations. Strangely, it had been determined the pilots for those crafts appeared to be human. Stranger still was the fact that all three possessed the same face, that of Captain Dodd. The emergency management directors of sixteen different agencies could only agree on one thing. It would take days if not weeks to get a full accounting of the dead and injured. All area hospitals, police and fire departments were in 24/7 emergency operations until further notice. School gymnasiums were converted to emergency field hospitals and shelters for the displaced.

Every military organization in every country was placed on alert, leaves were cancelled and food distribution points that already were in existence had been activated. Michael Rourke declared Hawaii in a state of National Disaster. In the affected areas, teams were removing building occupants along evacuation routes to primary assembly points and redirecting building occupants to stairs and exits away from the fire. Contingency plans for hazardous material spills or releases, nuclear power plant incidents, transportation accidents and everything else one could imagine had been activated.

The first forty-eight hours were the worst. Reports had been spotty and in-accurate. Initial responders were met with devastation and death. Those that died quickly from the flames of incineration were lucky. Those trapped under tons of collapsed buildings took days to die in slow agony without water, without food and totally alone.

Emma started having contractions shortly after the battle, but nature stepped in and the baby was safe and the doctors felt she could carry the child full term. Burns to John Rourke's left hand and arm were healing but the damage to Phillip Greene's jaw would take longer. With his face discolored and his mouth wired shut, Greene was avoiding the media and would be for quite a while.

*****

200 miles above the continent of Antarctica, within the formation of the KI ships, the tabloid was being monitored. The Captain was almost smiling, he thought, *"This could actually work out to our benefit. This could very easily be the best thing that could have happened for us."* It was time to begin...

Author's Note from Bob Anderson

I took a kick to the gut the morning of Wednesday, July 25th, 2012. I had sent a note to my friend Jerry Ahern's wife, Sharon—we had been working on a couple of projects. When she responded she told me that Jerry had passed peacefully in his sleep the night before.

To those of us that faithfully followed John Thomas Rourke, Jerry Ahern was special! I had the privilege of meeting Jerry back in 1993. I had called Ahern Enterprises (Jerry and Sharon's Holster Company) to order a holster for my custom .45 auto (the Widow Maker). After speaking with the "tech guy" for about 20 minutes he said, "If it doesn't work, send it back and we'll fix it."

I said, "I appreciate that, but I've heard it before—who am I speaking to?"

"Jerry Ahern," was his response.

"No s**t," was mine.

I was heading to the Air Force First Sergeant's Academy for training and we made arrangements to meet in Jerry's home town at the time, Commerce, GA. As I was sitting, waiting to meet Jerry I realized I had no idea of what he looked like. Just then a black pickup pulls in and a guy wearing a dark pair of aviator sun glasses and a bomber jacket (the same garb John Thomas Rourke wore) stepped out; I knew it was him.

Over the years, we developed a camaraderie I shall always treasure. He was an absolute gentleman and an absolute gentle man. Every phone conversation ended with his appellation, "God Bless" and he meant it.

I knew Jerry had been experiencing some health issues but his focus was always on the future, he began talking about bringing John Thomas Rourke back to life, revitalizing that series.

My story with THE SURVIVALIST began in late 1981, my father had passed away on Valentine's Day and we had moved back from Arkansas to Bossier City, Louisiana to be closer to my mom. Not having the benefit of a lot of money and having the curse of being an active reader, I traded paperbacks a lot at the Book Rack.

One day I came across THE SURVIVALIST #1 written by someone named Jerry Ahern. I picked it up but I initially thought it looked like something dealing with militias and neo-Nazis; there had been several episodes with those folks in Arkansas; I put the book back. Over the next several months, I kept encountering that book. Finally in 1982 I took a chance and bought it; by the end of the first chapter I was hooked!

When Jerry first mentioned to me that he was considering bringing the series back to life, I was thrilled and promised to help in any way I could. We discussed several story lines and I focused on research for him, little realizing how important that research would be to me in just a few months. When Sharon sent me word of his passing, she said, "Jerry died yesterday in his sleep—not what an action adventure writer envisions—but, he was a peaceful guy at heart." Personally, I think he did it right.

Sharon sent me two documents he had begun for the story. I don't remember ever having such dynamic emotions sweep over me. I was intimated, I was overwhelmed reading his last writings. The task of bringing John Thomas Rourke back to life was daunting. Jerry's story lines, several going on simultaneously in each book, his attention to detail, his knowledge of tactics and weapons all combined to form the most demanding and challenging writing assignment I ever received.

Honoring Jerry, honoring John Thomas and his family, bringing the story both back to life for past readers and trying to appeal to new readers was my challenge. Many times, I found in this attempt that Bob Anderson didn't know where the story was going. I would like to think that at those times, Jerry took over the keyboard and told the story for me. Jerry Ahern was a gentleman that didn't gripe or complain. I think, if I may speak for my buddy, he would say, "My only regret is not being with Sharon, my kids and grandkids."

I submit this effort to you, Jerry's readers and will close the way Jerry ended every phone call we ever had... God Bless.

Made in the USA
Lexington, KY
02 June 2013